HEARTS ON FIRE 7: CLAIMING CATALINA

Dixie Lynn Dwyer

MENAGE EVERLASTING

Siren Publishing, Inc.
www.SirenPublishing.com

A SIREN PUBLISHING BOOK
IMPRINT: Ménage Everlasting

HEARTS ON FIRE 7: CLAIMING CATALINA
Copyright © 2016 by Dixie Lynn Dwyer

ISBN: 978-1-68295-302-0

First Printing: May 2016

Cover design by Les Byerley
All art and logo copyright © 2016 by Siren Publishing, Inc.

Printed in the U.S.A.

PUBLISHER
Siren Publishing, Inc.
www.SirenPublishing.com

DEDICATION

Dear readers,

Thank you for purchasing this legal copy of *Claiming Catalina*.

Catalina is fighting the attraction she feels even though she wants to believe that meeting Cody, Jeremy, Don, and Cooper was just bad timing. They meet again, and because of her past, and a previous relationship with another man who broke her heart and betrayed her, she isn't sure if she should give the relationship a chance.

Have you ever had that first encounter, the one where your belly quivers and your heart races, and every sense in your body is on alert because the man you met is that appealing and perfect for you?

Despite spending some time together and learning about that person you, question the sincerity of love, the future of such a man's existence in your life and even question whether it was right, or would last?

So does Catalina until she focused on the most obvious method of figuring it out. She followed her heart. She remembered from day one meeting them in the ER and feeling her heart warm and her insides react. One look, a few exchanged words, and, indeed, they'd set her heart on fire. It was a flame that would burn forever because true love had the power to make it through everything.

May you enjoy her story.

Happy reading,

Hugs!

~Dixie~

HEARTS ON FIRE 7: CLAIMING CATALINA

DIXIE LYNN DWYER
Copyright © 2016

Prologue

"You are going to do that 10K race in two weeks, aren't you?" Shayla asked Catalina Shay as she stopped her bike next to where Catalina stood, her hands on her knees as she caught her breath.

Catalina was up to fifteen miles, but she wasn't sure it was good enough for the 10K race through and around Treasure Town and Fairway, the town over.

"I don't know. I'm still kind of slow, and I would hate to do it and not come in somewhere in the top ten."

"I think you will do fantastic. You've been training for it. Just sign up already. I'll even go with you to the Y so you can register today."

Catalina stood up and smiled at Shayla. She was a nurse at the Fairway General Hospital, too. She stretched out and Shayla got off her bike.

"Are you coming out with us tonight or what?" Shayla asked her.

She shrugged, not really feeling too enthusiastic about hitting the Station again. Although most of her good friends hung out there, she wasn't quite feeling like going.

"I don't know. This is my only night off for the rest of the week."

"All you do is work. You even cover other people's shifts all the time. You're going to get burned out," Shayla told her as they strolled down the walkway and through the park.

"I don't have anything better to do, and I love working in the ER."

"I know, and you're great at it, too, but you also work the burn unit sometimes and help out other days and even nights. You're the one who said you had no social life."

She exhaled. "I don't." She thought about Jeremy Jones and his brothers Cody, Don, and Cooper. She'd met them months ago at the hospital when Sophia had been abducted and seriously hurt. Jeremy and his brothers had helped to save Sophia's life. She had been surprised when she felt the instant attraction to the four brothers. It was obvious that they'd liked her, too, but they didn't live in New Jersey. They were also pretty secretive about their lives, especially Jeremy. He had been whisked off by some federal agents a short time after, and she'd never seen them again. That was just her luck, to finally meet men she was attracted to, but they weren't attracted to her. It would never work out. Being a workaholic was her life.

"Are you even listening to me?"

She looked at Shayla. "Yes, of course I am. I'm just tired from running fourteen miles. I think I'm going to head home to shower and then do some food shopping and clean up the townhouse."

"Oh, that sounds like loads of fun. How about I pick you up at six? We can meet MaryAnn and Destiny at the Boathouse for dinner before we check out the hot, single guys at the Station."

Catalina felt that nervous sensation hit her belly. It was as if she was losing her self-confidence when it came to men. There were plenty of guys that hit on her, but no one she felt attracted to.

She began to decline when Shayla shook her head.

"No, no, no. I will be at your house at six, and you better have your ass ready."

Catalina shook her head and exhaled. "Fine," she replied, and Shayla smiled wide as they got to the parking lot.

When Catalina finally got home after hitting the supermarket, she was feeling exhausted. She glanced at the clock and she knew she wouldn't have time to clean the condo. It wasn't as though it was dirty, but it gave her something to do on her days off. A glance around the room once she put away all the shopping and she saw that it really didn't need cleaning at all.

She headed to her bedroom and then grabbed a towel and her robe. She could lie down for a couple of hours and then fix her hair and makeup. She wasn't in the mood for this tonight, but it was better than sitting home alone. Lately, anything, even working, was better than sitting home alone. Tonight, like every other night, would be a waste of time. She'd rather focus her energy on the things that made her happy and were fulfilling, like being an ER nurse. That was worth her time and even giving up her days off.

* * * *

"Why is it so crowded tonight, and who the hell are all these guys?" MaryAnn asked then took a sip from her sangria.

"There's some sort of training going on in town for the next few weeks. Firefighters from across the country are here learning about new types of equipment and things. It's at the large convention center," Destiny told them, and then checked out two guys who walked by and winked at the three of them.

"Jesus, we can so get lucky tonight," Shayla stated, and they chuckled.

"You said three weeks? We can be pretty damn happy for a few weeks' worth of sexy men who aren't from around here," MaryAnn said to them, and they laughed.

Destiny looked at Catalina. "Did you hear about the new position in the hospital for an LPN? I caught wind of it today at work. Fantastic salary and a regular eight-to-four shift, off weekends, and paid vacation time and holidays off."

"No, what the hell kind of position is it?" Shayla asked her, and Catalina sat forward to hear, too.

"The requirements list a series of things from ER experience, the burn unit, critical care, pediatrics, and some certificate most people don't have. I heard from Mary Lang that the hospital offered the paid certificate classes to everyone, but only one nurse took advantage of it. So whoever that was, if she has the other experience, she would be the perfect candidate."

"Shit, well, there goes me applying. I didn't take that course. It was over a year ago and on Sunday nights. By Sunday, I'm trying to recover enough from Saturday to work Monday and the rest of the week. I sure didn't want to take some lame, boring class," Shayla said.

"It wasn't boring. It had a lot to do with medical financing and getting grants that could be used for individuals, as well as the hospital as a whole," Catalina told them and then took a small sip from her glass of wine.

"You were the one who took the course?" Shayla asked, sounding shocked.

"Oh my God, Catalina, I thought of you when I saw the requirements listed. You have most of the things and that certification no one else has. You should apply for it," Destiny told her.

"You totally have to. Do you realize how much of a normal life you could have working the day shifts and no more weekends or even midnights? Jesus. You should have made me take the course with you. Why didn't you tell me you were taking it?" Shayla asked.

"You were seeing Rourke at the time. Need I say more?" Catalina asked as she raised one of her eyebrows at Shayla. Shayla shook her head and then took a sip from her glass.

"He was ages ago, and I was stupid," Shayla said.

MaryAnn touched her arm and gave her a sympathetic expression. "You thought you loved him, and he was a manipulative asshole like most men."

"Yeah, we wouldn't remind you about how you gave us up for him and how he made you stop talking to us for over a month," Destiny added.

"Okay, there's no need to bring this up now. As I said, that was ages ago. So what's the salary for this job, and are they looking to hire from within, or are they considering transfers from out of state?"

"They're considering anyone that has all the requirements, Catalina. You should check it out and apply," Destiny told her.

"I don't know. I love working the ER. Some of the craziest times are during the night shifts, and the holidays are always nuts. I like to keep really busy and feel like I'm truly helping," Catalina told them.

"You work so damn hard. You deserve a great job and the salary starts at ninety thousand. There are bonuses and then raises as well, based on job performance. I bet if you were to get those grants and work out bringing in money to the hospital, you would get paid even more."

"You'd be crazy not to do it. If you did meet some guy or guys you liked, you wouldn't have to worry about your work schedule and trying to make time for them," Shayla said to her.

"Well, my luck with men has not been great, and considering that I haven't dated a man since college, I'd say I don't need to use having time for a guy as incentive to apply for a job, but thanks for the vote of confidence."

"Catalina?"

* * * *

They all turned to look up, and Catalina's mouth dropped, and her heart instantly began to race. Cooper, Jeremy's brother, was standing there, and a huge smile broke out on his face as she locked gazes with him.

"Cooper? What are you doing here?" She stood up. He smiled as he gently placed his hands on her upper arms and leaned forward to kiss her cheek. She was stunned at the sensations she felt and couldn't help but to look around for his brothers.

He stepped back and placed his hands in his pockets. He looked like some sexy Ralph Lauren Polo model, but with extra-large muscles and a sexy, flirty grin.

"Don and I are in town for the next few weeks doing this training thing at the convention center."

"Oh, great," Catalina said and then heard Shayla clear her throat. She turned to look at them all smirking and waiting for an introduction.

"Oh, Cooper, meet my friends Shayla, MaryAnn, and Destiny."

Copper smiled and shook their hands, and her friends ate him up with their eyes. He was that damn sexy. She felt the twinge of jealousy, and then her friends stood up.

"We need some more drinks. Why don't we head to the bar and you two can talk here at the table and catch up?" Shayla said to them.

"You don't have to leave. My brother Don is around here somewhere, and a few other guys we met with the McCallister brothers," Cooper told them, but then he looked right at Catalina.

"Here, take my seat. I need to use the lady's room," Destiny told him, and her three friends left her standing there all alone with Cooper.

"I didn't mean to scare them away," he said, and she took a seat. He took the seat next to her, and his knee bumped her thigh. Their gazes locked.

"They were looking for excuses to go meet some guys," she told him and then looked around for her friends, but they were nowhere in sight.

"Were you planning on doing that, too?" he asked, scooting closer to her. It was pretty loud in the place and very crowded. She held his gaze and absorbed dark brown eyes and that flirty, sexy expression that made her feel all giddy inside.

"No. I didn't even want to come here tonight."

"Why not?" he asked her, and seemed really interested, as though he wasn't just trying to force a conversation.

"I really don't like to hang out at bars, and I'm so busy working all the time that I kind of like to enjoy my day off."

"What do you like to do when you're not working in the ER and patching up bullet wounds?" He winked.

"How is your brother's arm? It healed okay? Didn't leave too bad of a scar?"

"I wouldn't know," he said to her and then looked away a moment.

She sensed something was wrong, but she really didn't know Cooper well enough to ask him. She had helped Jeremy at the hospital that day.

"I thought you guys lived together," she said.

He leaned back slightly and held her gaze. He had one hand on the table and the other over the back of her chair. He was close enough that she could smell his cologne and relish his masculinity.

"We do now, but with his job and working undercover for the past few years, we kind of drifted apart a little. We've been working on getting to know one another again. He was gone for almost three years."

"My God, that must have been rough on him, leaving his family, his brothers, and having to pretend to be someone else for so long."

"I guess so. I mean, I understand his job was intense and required him to be secretive, but the four of us have always done things together. We had a plan, and we all chose to stay within New York and around our parents, and then he gets into his profession and is asked to go deep undercover. It was like one day he was there, and the next, we get one five-minute phone call telling all of us to pretend he's dead and not to look him up or try to find him because of his job. He thought it might take a year, but then one year passed, then another, and one day he calls up and needs our help."

"And you were there for him. So that bond you have is obviously strong. Three years apart, and one phone call for help and you all leaped into action. That's damn special." She felt her heart grow heavy. The tears reached her eyes, and she looked away. She had a sister, and they barely talked to one another.

"Hey, you okay? I didn't mean to get you all depressed with my frigged-up family shit."

"Are you kidding me? Your family doesn't sound frigged up. They sound strong and supportive. My family, on the other hand, is frigged up." She smirked, and he chuckled.

"That bad?" he asked.

"I have a sister I haven't even spoken to in over six years." She played with the stem of her empty wine glass.

"A falling-out?" he asked, and when she went to answer, C.C. came over.

"Can I get you two something to drink from the bar?" the waitress asked.

"Sure thing. Catalina, another white wine?" he asked, and she nodded, and then he ordered a Bud. Catalina smiled at C.C., the new waitress at the Station. She was very sweet and kept to herself.

She watched Cooper say hello and shake some guy's hand who walked by. He gave him a nod, looked at Catalina, and then winked at Cooper.

"Hey, it's Catalina, right?" the guy said to her. She nodded.

"You took care of me about six months back when I wound up in the ER with a ruptured spleen from a fall during a fire."

"Oh, yes, I remember you. How are you feeling? Wait, you also had appendicitis, too, right?" she asked.

He smiled and placed a hand on the back of her chair. She thought she saw Cooper's expression change. He appeared angry, but then the guy squatted down lower. He held her gaze.

"It's Michael, and yes, you figured that out pretty damn quick or I could have died. There were, like, six burn victims in the ER at the time and chaos everywhere, but you stayed with me. I never got the chance to thank you, honey. You were amazing." He took her hand, brought it to his lips, and kissed it. She felt a bit embarrassed, but then Cooper cleared his throat.

"Well, you said your thank-you, but Catalina and I were in the middle of a conversation, so if you don't mind?" Cooper told him.

Michael stood back up and nodded. "See ya around, Catalina. I'll see you tomorrow, Cooper." He then took off.

"That was weird," she said to Cooper, who took a slug from the beer CC had just dropped off along with the glass of white wine for Catalina.

Cooper looked her over. "Ever date any of the people you helped to save?" He sounded kind of annoyed or something.

"No, how about you?" she countered, giving it right back to him.

He leaned closer and held her gaze. She felt her belly twist and tighten. Even her nipples hardened he was so close, his breath warm, his gaze sexy.

"No."

She raised one of her eyebrows up at him. "Really? You expect me to believe that you've never hooked up with someone you helped save from a fire or from danger?"

"The question was date, not hook up with."

"Oh, so there's a big difference there, huh?"

"Well, hooking up is quick and easy. Dating involves a bit more commitment."

"That's true." She gave a small smirk before she took a sip from her wine. He just stared at her.

"Ever date or hook up with a soldier or a firefighter?" he asked.

"Nope."

They were silent a few moments, and she couldn't help but wonder what he was thinking. Then he smirked.

"Aren't you going to ask me if I've ever hooked up with or dated a nurse?"

She was taken back at his flirty forwardness, and her cheeks felt warm. She was suddenly so embarrassed. She shook her head.

He reached out and ran his finger along her jaw then clutched her chin.

"Well, I never did. Never knew someone for such a short time and felt so instantly attracted to her."

"Hmmm, use that line a lot?" she asked, but it came out sounding breathless instead of strong and confident.

"It's not a line. I've never said anything like that before. Does my honesty scare you, Catalina?" he asked, moving his lips closer.

"You don't scare me at all, Cooper." But as she said his name, he kissed her, and she was intrigued that it was so good she forgot they were in the middle of a crowded room, and at the Station, no less. He ran his hand along her shoulder and neck, deepening the kiss and then slowly pulling back as she began to pull back.

Speechless, they stared at one another, and then they both smiled.

"Damn, baby, I wanted to do that months ago when I first laid eyes on you in the ER waiting room."

She pulled back and then looked around, wondering if anyone saw them kiss. Sure enough, her friends had, and they were high-fiving one another then toasting her as they waved and winked. Cooper took that second to turn and look, and they all waved and hollered.

"Oh God, they're so embarrassing."

Cooper chuckled, but then covered her hand and caressed it.

"Maybe I get their approval."

"Or they're just a bunch of goofballs that had a few too many shots."

"I'm leaning toward the approval thing."

She chuckled. "Confident, huh?"

"Not confident enough to believe you'd make my fantasies come true and you'd come home with me tonight."

She was shocked, not only about him saying that to her but how easily her mind and body said yes.

"Oh, trying to fulfill the whole hooking-up-with-a-nurse thing so you have that covered, too?" she asked, and his eyes widened, and then he got very serious.

"Shit. That did sound like that, didn't it? Frig. I didn't mean it that way. I was just teasing. I'm sorry if I offended you."

She chuckled and covered his forearm with her hand. "Hey, forget about it. We were teasing one another."

"Cooper, there you are. I was looking all over the place for you."

Cooper looked up and smiled as Catalina turned around to see who it was. Her heart hammered, and she couldn't help but to stare in awe at Don, Cooper's brother. They looked like twins. His eyes widened, and then he smiled.

"Holy crap, you found Catalina."

He leaned down and gave her a kiss hello. "How are you, honey? Damn, you look good. No wonder he never came back to the table with the beers."

Don took the seat next to her, and Cooper smiled.

"What are you guys talking about?" Don asked.

"Oh, I was just asking Catalina to make my fantasies come true and come home with me tonight, but she's not biting." He winked.

She gave Cooper a smack. "Cooper!" she reprimanded, and Don gave her arm a little nudge, bringing her attention to him.

"Make all our fantasies come true and come home with us."

"Oh, brother, you guys are crazy. Stop teasing me." She chuckled and then took a sip of her wine, but as she lowered the glass, both men were staring at her. Cooper placed his hand on her knee and caressed it and a little higher while Don covered her hand that lay on the table.

"Who said we were teasing?" Don asked, rendering her, speechless.

* * * *

Cooper couldn't believe their luck, to actually bump into Catalina, the one woman who'd grabbed him and his brothers' attention months ago. It had been bad timing. Hell, even now was bad timing, and they lived over an hour away right now, but things were changing. They were all trying to work out spending more time together. They'd had a few years apart from Jeremy, and it had weighed on their relationship and bond, but the last few months, they'd made progress. There wasn't that strange sensation anymore of not really knowing who Jeremy was and whether he still was interested in sharing a life with them and even settling down.

But there were things to work out, and until he opened up entirely to them and let them in on his fears, his quiet thoughts, they wouldn't be able to move on together.

Sitting here so close to Catalina, a gorgeous woman with her long, blonde hair and deep blue eyes, and feeling possessive, Cooper found was becoming hard to resist.

He held her gaze. His brother was feeling it, too. Don was pressed up against her chair, his arm over hers, his hand covering Catalina's dainty one.

"Does this scare you? Meeting us here like this after not seeing us for a few months?"

"And then us asking you to come home with us?" Don added.

She looked from Cooper to Don and then swallowed hard. She lowered her eyes, and he could see she was struggling, too.

"It's not as scary as you may think. I don't know why, but when you asked, the word yes was on the tip of my tongue."

He smiled softly. His heart pounded.

"But…" she said, and he felt his excitement deflate, "I'm not that kind of woman. I don't know either of you. We haven't seen one another in months. You disappeared, and you live over an hour away. It just wouldn't work, and I don't do one-night stands." She slowly pulled her hand from Don's, turned her legs so Cooper's hand fell from her knee, and then she smiled.

"Well, I think the smart thing to do right now is to go back to my friends and hang out with them. I have to get up early for work tomorrow anyway, but it was nice seeing you both again," she said, sounding so sad and looking hurt.

Cooper couldn't let her leave. "Wait." He stood up as she did. So did Don.

"We're working in town for the next few weeks. Maybe we could spend some time together. Maybe do lunch or dinner?" he suggested.

"I'm on nights for the next several days. I need to sleep during the day," she told him.

Don moved around to stand in front of her, too. She was short compared to them. She was five foot four tops, and next to their six-foot-three frames, she was small, and he felt protective.

"You have to eat, though. We could meet you at any time. In fact, the evenings before you head to the hospital would be great since we're running the training facility this week," Cooper added.

"I'll see."

Cooper pulled out his cell phone. "What's your cell number? I'll send you a text with our numbers, and we can try to coordinate."

She exhaled, and he knew his persistence had won her over as she rambled off her number. He texted her right away, and she reached into her purse and pulled out her cell phone. He smiled.

"We'll call you this week."

"Bye," she whispered and looked at them both, but before she could walk away, Cooper placed a hand on her waist to stop her. She paused, and he wrapped his arm around her waist and slowly pulled her toward him, wondering if she would shove him away and hoping she would allow him to kiss her again.

As he pulled her close, he pressed his lips to her temple and then her ear.

"I look forward to seeing you again, Catalina. Please give this a try." As he slowly pulled back, he brushed his lips over hers. Then he gave her a wink and a smile.

"Goodnight." She then glanced at Don, who took her hand and brought it to his lips, kissing the top of it.

"See you soon," Don said, and they both watched her walk away toward the bar and her friends.

The way her round ass swayed, so sexy in that skirt, had his cock super hard and his mind imagining what she looked like naked. The attraction he felt was so instant and powerful. He couldn't ignore this feeling, and one look at Don and he knew his brother wanted her, too. His arms were crossed in front of his chest, and a serious expression fell over his face. One look over his shoulder and Cooper saw the guys talking to Catalina and her friends. Two of the men were awfully close to Catalina.

"Damn, she's special. I can't believe you kissed her. I wish she'd said yes to coming home with us, but I guess knowing she isn't into one-night stands just makes her more appealing."

"She sure is. We all felt an attraction to her that day at the hospital months ago. Maybe this is our chance, Don. Maybe Catalina could be the woman we all share who completes our family."

Don placed his hand on Cooper's shoulder. "I don't think we should jump the gun. It might be just the two of us with her and not the others. Jeremy is still holding back and not quite adjusting to being out of the agency, and Cody has been a beast lately with the terrorist threats and the case he's working on."

"But if we don't make the time for a woman, for Catalina, then we could lose her entirely. We're at different points in our lives than our brothers. They're more than ready to make the changes and settle down, but they just can't seem to give up that control and need to stay on top of their game."

Jeremy had lost his position in the agency because his identity was revealed, but he was able to keep his job as an agent, even though he wasn't happy. Until he found something to replace his old job, he would be difficult to live with.

Cody was getting burned out in his position. With all the new regulations and rules, it seemed like terrorists actually had rights, and by the time they all followed procedure, the element of surprise was lost and so was the opportunity to arrest the evildoers. It was a vicious cycle, and the stress of it all showed lately on Cody's face and in his attitude. The more Cooper thought about things, the more he felt as though maybe sharing a woman together might not ever happen. So why shouldn't he and Don entertain their attraction to Catalina? That was if they could get her to see them again. Maybe they'd pushed too hard considering they hadn't seen her in months.

"Hey, what's the pissed-off expression for?" Don asked.

"Just thinking that maybe we shouldn't have said anything about taking her home with us. In fact, I can't believe I actually said that to her. I didn't even think. I just followed what was going on in my head and how excited I was to see her again. I acted like a fucking horny high school kid."

Don chuckled then took a slug from his beer. "I said it to her, too, and I didn't even kiss her."

Cooper looked around for her and spotted her in the same place, but her eyes locked onto his before she quickly turned away.

"God, I hope she answers our call when we ask her out."

"I hope so, too. There's just something about her."

"Hey, what happened? You two crash and burn with Catalina?" Ice asked as he showed up behind them. Cooper gave him a sideways expression, and Ice chuckled.

"Don't feel defeated. She doesn't take up any guys on any offers. Gets really annoyed when guys act like she'll go home with them just because she was friendly."

Cooper felt like such an asshole.

"What's her deal?" Don asked. "I mean, you sound like you know her well."

"She's one of Serefina's best friends. She and her crew hang out a lot, although not much lately. Catalina works a lot."

"No boyfriend, then?" Don asked, and Ice smirked.

"You guys interested, huh?"

"Maybe," Cooper said to him, and Ice chuckled.

"Well, that might not work, considering you live over an hour away, unless the two of you are considering the job offer from the Board. I know it's nowhere as intense as New York City, but you're getting older. Maybe slowing it down and moving to a nice, peaceful town like Treasure Town would be filled with positive opportunities." Ice took a slug from his beer bottle.

"We haven't had too much time to discuss the job offer or look into the details. Plus, we have Cody and Jeremy to think about. They're not sure what they want to do with their jobs," Don said.

"Well, when an opportunity presents itself, you should at least consider it, talk it over with them, and perhaps see if now is a good time to move. You know you already have a lot of friends here, never mind professional connections and relationships. You'd all fit in just fine."

"Well, it's something to consider, and I guess Don and I have some things to discuss since the job offer was for both of us. We'll let you know," Cooper told Ice.

Ice raised his beer bottle. "To hoping you'll join the family here in Treasure Town."

They clicked bottles and smiled as Cooper wondered if maybe it truly was the right time to move out of New York, slow down the pace a bit. But as he glanced back toward Catalina, he wondered if he was just dreaming, being hopeful, maybe even desperate to achieve their dreams of being one family. He hardly even knew the woman, but she was the first one he'd met that ever made his mind fast-forward to a serious commitment. That in itself was definitely something he needed to explore further.

As he felt a hand slap on his back and a group of young firefighters join them, offering beers, he had to put all thoughts on hold and talk shop with the locals. Tomorrow would be a different story.

Chapter 1

"So, spill the beans, missy. What the heck happened between you, Don, and Cooper last night at the Station?" Serefina asked as Catalina sat in the break room, trying to drink a cup of coffee as she spoke on the phone.

"What are you talking about? There are no beans to spill." Catalina rubbed her temple on her right side, as she used her shoulder to hold the phone, since her other hand held the cup of coffee. Instantly, her neck ached.

"Come on, really? I've known you forever. You were immediately attracted to the four of them."

"They don't live in New Jersey, never mind anywhere near Treasure Town. It would never work out. Plus, only Cooper and Don were at the Station last night. We talked, and I'm on nights all week."

"Well, that didn't stop you from kissing Cooper, from what I heard."

"Jeesh! Did everyone see the man kiss me?"

"Oh my God, you like him. I knew it. So when are you going to see them?"

"Duh. I'm not going to. It's a waste of time. I can't get involved with some one-night stand or some free-for-all sexcapade."

"Catalina, you like them, and they like you. Maybe it can work. Ice told me that Cooper and Don were offered these great jobs with the county running the fire training facility and programs for every fire house. It's a pretty great opportunity. They might move here, then what?"

"Well, I'm happy for them, but considering that they both asked me to go home with them last night, and I hardly know them, I'd say they weren't looking for the commitment-type of woman."

"Damn, they asked you that straight out? It must have been a hell of a kiss," Serefina said, and Catalina exhaled as she leaned back against the small couch.

"It was freaking incredible. I swear if I were easy, or didn't think I would ever see them again, I would have said yes."

"Damn, that's amazing, but maybe it's not what you think. Maybe he just blurted it out because he was so very attracted to you."

"But then Don came over and added the same thing. It just seemed like that's what they do—like a woman, feel an attraction, and then take her home to screw her. I'm not like that and never have been. I want more, Serefina, and it's starting to feel like I'm never going to get that around here."

"Hey, don't say that. When the time is right, you'll meet the right guy or guys. Just hold steady. How is work going, anyway?"

"Well, I heard about this new position. It would mean no more night shifts. I could actually get a tan." She chuckled.

"Is it in the hospital or elsewhere?" Serefina asked, and Catalina could tell she was worried. As much as Catalina thought about moving and starting fresh somewhere, she loved the town and the people too much.

"It's here and with the ER still, and entails a lot of responsibility, but the benefits seem awesome."

"So you're going to apply for it?"

"Maybe. I'll decide soon."

"You should go for it. Maybe this is the change you need, and it can free up your nights so you can go out more."

"I'm thinking about it. A change could be a really good thing right now. We'll see. I'd better get going. I'll talk to you soon."

"You bet. Be safe."

"Always," Catalina said and then disconnected the call.

The second she did, the door pushed open.

"We just got a call. Five victims, multiple-car pileup, on their way now," one of the other nurses told her. She immediately stood up, tossed her half-full coffee cup into the garbage, and headed out the door to the ER. Time to go back to work. Her fifteen-minute break was now over.

* * * *

The phone rang several times, but no voice message came on. Don looked at Cooper. "Are you sure she gave us her real cell number?"

"Bro, she was right there when it went off. It's hers. Maybe the voicemail is full," Cooper said as they both sat at the table in the kitchen.

"Or she's avoiding our call again. It's been a week. Last night should have been her last night shift."

"Maybe if we go to the Station tonight, we'll see her there with her friends?"

"Maybe. I guess we'll head out to Sullivan's for lunch and then check out those two houses for sale. If we're seriously going to consider moving, I want to have a nice place and all the details planned out so that when we talk to Cody and Jeremy, they can't say they're not interested."

"Sounds like a plan. Let's go."

As they headed down the road in their Jeep, Don thought about why Catalina was avoiding them. Sure, if things got serious, it would be hard to have a long-distance relationship, but the woman wasn't even giving them a chance. Why was that? Had something happened to her to make her decline their interest? Maybe he was reading into things. Or maybe he felt a bit off-kilter and insulted because not once in his life had a woman declined an offer of coming home with him, a date, or even a kiss. Shit. She wasn't even their woman, and she was making his head spin.

As Cooper pulled along the curb and into an open parking spot, Don spotted some guys talking to a blonde. Her back was toward him, but he could tell she had a great figure in the slim-fitting blue sundress she wore, and she was carrying a large bag on her shoulder. When she turned away from the one guy closest to her, Don caught sight of the low V of the dress and how her breasts nearly poured from the top, yet the outfit looked stylish and classy, like something a model would wear.

"Holy shit." He took in the full sight of her and then her face. Despite the dark black sunglasses she wore, he could tell right away that it was Catalina.

"Is that Catalina?" Cooper asked as he got out of the Jeep.

"Sure as shit is."

"Who the fuck is she with?"

"I don't know, but looks like she's not with them. She's trying to pass by them," Don said, and he and Cooper made their way closer.

From Don's perspective, Catalina appeared annoyed as she placed her hand on her hip and started raising her voice.

"I said I'm not interested, so take a hike."

"That's our cue," Don said. "Hey, baby, we've been looking all over for you. We were worried." Don moved right between the guys there, practically knocking them over. Cooper stood with his arms crossed in a mean, protective stance.

"Are you bothering our woman?" he barked.

Catalina gasped, but Don pulled her close and squeezed her hip as he wrapped an arm around her waist, bringing her closer to Cooper and him.

"Your woman? Shit. If she were mine, she would never be left alone," one guy said, and he sounded a little drunk.

"Well, she isn't yours, so get lost. The lady isn't interested."

The four men looked at Catalina.

"See you around, doll, when your muscle-head boyfriends aren't around," one of them stated.

"Hey, you fucking ever come near her again and you'll answer to me. Got it?" Cooper stated firmly as he stepped toward them, ready to fight.

The one drunk guy raised his hands up. "Whatever. We're out of here."

They started walking away, and Don couldn't help but to pull Catalina close and hug her. "Are you okay?" he asked, and she nodded.

"I was just coming from the phone store. I was walking out, and these guys followed me and starting bothering me. It was so weird. I'm sorry that you had to get involved." She began to pull away.

He held her by her hips and stared down into her eyes. "We were pissed when we saw you talking to those guys."

"Yeah, especially since we called and left multiple messages on your cell phone asking about getting together," Don added.

"You did? Oh God, I'm so sorry. My stupid phone got broken on Tuesday night at work. The ER was super busy, and when multiple victims of a car accident came in at once, it was pandemonium to get to everyone in a timely manner. As we were working, one of the new nurses hadn't locked the gurney and it started to collapse. I grabbed onto the corner as the others helped, but my cell phone popped out of my back pocket and broke. Working all these night shifts all week, I hadn't had time during the day to bring it to get fixed because I was sleeping. So, sorry." She finally exhaled.

Don leaned forward and softly kissed her lips. "You're forgiven," he whispered after he pulled away.

She pulled back. "Don, I told you guys that this wasn't a good idea." She was obviously taken aback that he'd kissed her like that.

"We think otherwise. Besides, it's fate us meeting like this again." He winked then released her from around the waist and took her hand.

"I agree, and we missed a whole week we could have spent getting to know you. We're headed to Sullivan's for lunch. Want to join us?" Don asked as Cooper took up position on her other side.

"I really shouldn't."

"Oh, yes, you should," Don said as he looked over her breasts in the dress she wore and then moved his gaze to her lips and eyes.

"Please? It's our treat," Cooper added and winked.

"You two are definitely persistent, and you did just save me from getting into a confrontation with four drunk guys."

"That we are. Just wait," Cooper teased, and the three of them headed to Sullivan's to eat lunch.

* * * *

Catalina was a bit embarrassed as they entered the restaurant and saw so many of her friends and, of course, Cooper and Don's new friends, now that they had been teaching and training at the fire training building. Everyone said hello and shook hands, gave hugs, and, of course, assumed they were an item. Truth was, she didn't mind fantasizing it was true at all. Cooper and Don were gorgeous and extralarge. Their muscles had muscles, and they were seriously attractive. Being this close as they sat at a small table and the men flanked her on either side, she saw the deep similarities in them.

"Are you two twins?" she asked them. Both of them smiled at the same time and exactly the same. She chuckled. "That is very cool."

"Yep, I'm older," Cooper told her as he reached up and pressed a strand of hair away from her neck and her breasts. He looked her over and then pulled his bottom lip between his teeth as if looking at her was driving him wild. Well, looking at him and Don, feeling them this close, was pretty damn arousing, too.

"By two minutes, Cooper. That's nothing," Don said as he placed his arm over the back of her chair.

"Two minutes is a lot of time," Cooper added.

Catalina chuckled. "So, do you two tend to fight a lot?" she asked as the waitress came over to take their drink orders. They all ordered sweet tea and then continued talking.

Catalina was laughing a lot. She was so surprised at how comfortable she was talking with Cooper and Don. They ate their lunches continuing to talk non-stop.

"How is the fire training program you both are running, going?" She took a sip from her sweet tea, leaning back against Don's arm. He caressed her shoulder, and she didn't mind one bit. In fact, she felt that tingling sensation move along her spine and even between her legs.

"It's been going very well. There's a lot of information and techniques to teach, but everyone seems really diligent and focused," Cooper stated.

"Well, almost everyone," Don said, then took a sip from his glass. She looked at him, at his dark brown eyes and the serious expression on his face.

"Oh no, that sounds like you have a few students who aren't quite listening," she said to him.

"We have a handful of rookies and some seasoned firemen who think they know everything, but we've been taking them down a small notch at a time," Cooper said.

"Well, believe me, in every profession we have our share of the weaker links or people who think they know more than anyone else, and that actual experience matters. Like the story I told you guys earlier about my cell phone. This one particular nurse really thinks she knows it all. Another nurse and I have both told her to check the locks on the tables multiple times. She waved us off and, of course, nearly caused an accident that could have hurt a patient worse."

"Never mind your phone, which led us to believe you were blowing us off." Cooper reached up, cupped her chin, moved his lips closer to hers, and then kissed her lips softly.

Her eyes were still closed when their lips parted, and when she opened them, she caught him staring at her.

"God, Catalina, you're so beautiful and sweet. I'm so sorry if I came on too strong last week at the Station. I just, well, I never felt so much so instantly, and I let my stupid mouth say what flashed through my mind," Cooper admitted.

"We did, but we know you're not some easy woman or just some fling. We want to get to know you better. Today has been a lot of fun, and we feel comfortable," Don said as she looked at him.

He used his thumb to caress her lower lip, held her gaze, and began to lean closer. It was a moment of pull back or just let go and feel to see where this led. She didn't move at all, and then Don's lips touched hers, and she knew she was done for.

"You only have another week or so left here, right?" she asked a few minutes later as they argued over the bill, both Don and Cooper insisting they pay.

"Yes, but we have some decisions to make about a career opportunity right here in Treasure Town," Don explained.

"Yes, the position would be for the both of us, and we would have better hours than what we have in New York right now," Cooper said.

"We're both ready to slow down a bit now. We've been at this for years, first in the military and then the public sector. It becomes tiresome," Don added.

It made her wonder how old they were exactly. She was still young and maybe the difference in ages could be a problem.

"You make us sound so old, bro. You're scaring Catalina," Cooper said and smiled.

Her belly fluttered, and other parts became aroused. God, they were so big, so sexy and masculine that she could get lost in their embraces, but she'd never been with more than one man before. If things went wrong, she could be ruined forever.

"Sorry. It's just that you get to a point where you know in your career or profession that it's time to move on. Interests change. You think about the future and the things you thought you wanted and still want." Don took her hand from her lap and brought it to his lips as he kissed her knuckles and held her gaze.

"I understand what you mean. I've been debating about a possible career move, too. There's a position offered in the hospital where I work now, and it has a lot of positives. I can work a regular eight-to-four shift, off on holidays, even weekends, and get bonuses, paid vacation, and a bunch of other stuff all because of my experience and because I took a bunch of special certification classes over the last two years."

"It sounds great. What's holding you back?" Cooper asked her.

"To be honest, I guess, like you guys, I've been thinking that a change is needed, but I was leaning toward leaving town."

"What?" Don asked, squeezing her hand a little tighter.

"Well, it was my thought process for a while because nothing new was happening in my life, I've been working like a dog, have no social life, and it seems like everyone around me is moving on and expanding on their lives and achievements and I'm just standing still. I don't know. It sounds lame, I'm sure," she said, lowering her head.

"No, actually you sound a lot like we did a few months ago, and even how Cody and Jeremy sound now when they talk about leaving their jobs," Cooper told her.

She looked at him. "They want to leave their jobs?"

"They're involved with heavy, stressful careers that entail a lot of secrecy and bad stuff. You know, bad people," Don added.

"I know. I was there when the men brought in Sophia, and I heard what Jeremy and the others did to rescue her. I could only imagine how dangerous their work must be."

"It's taken a toll on our relationship, too, in a lot of ways," Don admitted.

The waitress brought back their change and set it down. They said thank you, and then Cooper stood up. "Come walk with us. We can talk more privately outside on the boardwalk."

She stood up, grabbed her bag, and took his hand as the three of them left Sullivan's and waved at some friendly faces. She couldn't help but wonder what Don had meant when he said their jobs had taken a toll on their relationships. She wanted to ask, but maybe Don felt he shouldn't have made that last statement. The waitress coming over was the perfect excuse to drop it and leave.

But then Don stopped at the railing to the beach where it was empty and quiet.

She stood there looking out at the ocean, loving the smell of the salt water and the sound of waves rolling onto the shore and seagulls singing above.

Don stepped in behind her and placed his hand over one of her hands and the other arm wrapped around her midsection as she held the railing. She felt his hard, warm body press up against her ass and back, and it aroused her. His large, warm palm felt so good as it slid along her quivering belly and then against her hipbone in a possessive manner. He was so big and masculine, making her feel safe, dainty, secure in his cage of warmth. She couldn't help but to lean back, and Don kissed her shoulder, then her neck as Cooper came to stand right next to them, covering her other hand with his.

Being connected like this felt so good, and so right. It amazed her. She finally understood how her friends felt, the ones engaged in ménage relationships, and how content and happy they always looked. This was different, and the fact that it had happened so quickly, and instantly, amazed her.

"Coop and I have always been inseparable. We share everything, and we like it that way," he whispered as he kissed her neck and along her earlobe. She tilted her head up as his hand moved along her waist, as if wanting to feel her body, caress it, leave his imprint on it, before squeezing her against him as their lips touched. A moment later, Cooper was releasing her and Don was pulling her into his arms and kissing her deeply. It felt so good, and it was wild how she so naturally, easily, went from kissing one man to the next. It didn't feel strange or scary but, instead, empowering, sexy, and inspirational.

Don released her lips slowly and then stared down into her eyes.

"Baby, what you do to me."

"And me," Cooper added, pressing against her back and caressing her shoulders then down her arms.

"I feel it, too," she whispered and then wanted to kick herself for admitting that aloud, so soon, making herself vulnerable to these two men she barely knew.

"Don't be scared. We're going to take this slow because we don't want to fuck this up, but damn, you've got me wanting to take that job we were offered, move into Treasure Town, and begin a new life with you and my brothers," Don said, and she gasped. Her eyes widened, and she swallowed hard.

Cooper squeezed her shoulders.

"I think you just freaked her out," Cooper whispered, and then turned her around and pulled her into an embrace. She wrapped her arms around his midsection and hugged him back. A few moments of silence passed, and then Cooper turned her toward the water, keeping his arm wrapped around her as they faced the beach and ocean.

Don placed his hands on the railing and hung his head, looking so upset suddenly, and her heart ached for him. She reached out and ran her hand along his shoulder and arm. He shot his head toward her, appearing shocked at her empathetic response.

"My brothers and I have always talked about having the same relationship our parents do. Our mom is married to three men. They live in Connecticut. They're very happy, complete, and it's something we've wanted forever," Cooper told her.

"But our lives have taken different paths over the years, and it was only recently we got our brothers back," Don explained.

"You mean because of the incident with the federal government and Jeremy losing his undercover position?" she asked, knowing some of the details now that Sophia was hanging out with all of Catalina's friends.

"Yes, you see, we couldn't contact, speak to, or even know where Jeremy was for almost three years because of his deep undercover operation," Don said to her.

"God, that must have been so tough. How did you handle it?"

"Like good soldiers," Cooper said. "We fully absorbed ourselves in our jobs, our positions, but add in Cody doing secret shit and flying out of the country to capture terrorists, then even hunt some here on U.S. soil, and the last five years of our lives have been hell." Cooper squeezed her a little snugger against his body.

"We want you to understand something," Don said. "The way we all met you was so out of the blue, but when we saw you at the hospital, when you helped Jeremy, the attraction, the connection the four of us had to you was instant. We all locked gazes and it was like we knew. I know it sounds crazy, how quickly our minds our expectations are running in full force, but this is real. I…we've never felt like this."

"Maybe you just wanted that to happen," she suggested. Don shook his head, and then Cooper turned her around and pressed her against the railing with his hands on either side of her waist, trapping her in. He stared down into her eyes, and she saw, she felt, the intensity in his dark brown eyes. He shook his head.

"No. It was real. It was instant, and they even talked about you a few times afterwards."

"But their jobs are making them crazy," Don said. "Cody is ready to quit. He's had it with the new protocols and how these criminal terrorists seem to have rights. Jeremy is at his wit's end trying to handle a desk job and inside intelligence instead of fieldwork and being an agent. It's like they feel worthless and unsure of a future and what they could have. It's a hard transitional time for them, and they won't talk about shit." Don ran his fingers through his hair.

"You can't force them to get through it. It's obvious from what you explained that both Cody and Jeremy love their jobs and don't want to let go. They were probably very good at them, too, and feel that if they move on, if they try something different and something goes wrong, that they could have possibly stopped it. I get that way all the time working in the ER and covering extra shifts and hardly getting time off. I'm so worried that if I'm not there and something goes wrong, some other nurse with less experience, or maybe who is overtired or not on her game, might cause a person to be worse off. I don't know. I guess it's a control thing combined with a need to feel appreciated, important, and vital to every patient that enters the ER that I'm assigned to. So I get it."

Cooper gave a soft smile as he reached up and caressed her cheek.

"You do get it. You're special. We want you, Catalina," he said, and she could tell there was a "but" in there.

"But?" she whispered, feeling emotional and like they were going to turn her down because their brothers weren't on board and that was what they always wanted.

She couldn't help the sadness that filled her heart, which was so foolish, considering she'd known these men for such a short time, but that was her luck. Every so often she met a guy she felt attracted to, and then something went wrong or nothing came of it. She was starting to think it was her, that something was wrong with her because of Paul. She'd dated him in college and given her virginity and her heart to him, only for him to wind up using her. Paul had hurt her so badly. She could never forgive him. She didn't even know what she would do if she ever saw Paul again, which was pretty likely, living in a touristy town like this and him working in New York City. Lots of New Yorkers came here to vacation.

"But you need to know that Don and I want this to work out. We want more dates with you, more kisses, more feeling you in our arms and knowing you're our woman and no one else's. We want Cody and Jeremy involved with this relationship, too. We want to share you with them and all be together."

She felt uneasy about it, scared actually because it made her feel like an item, a possession. The warning signals went off, the fear that she could lose so much by taking this chance, especially with what had happened in college. Paul had ruined her ability to trust a man under normal circumstances, never mind under something as unique as a ménage relationship. She couldn't even believe they were talking like this so freely.

She looked away from them and pressed from his embrace. He released her, and she stood to the side and looked out toward the water.

"I don't think that's going to work. The fact that you want to share me, and both of you are right here, is one thing. I've never really thought I would get involved in a relationship like this, but you have to understand the risks are so great. You guys aren't even living in town. You're debating about a job transfer and change. Cody and Jeremy aren't even here. You don't know how they really feel, and this type of relationship can't be forced. I won't feel like a possession, a means to trying to mend the relationship you once had with your brothers."

"No, Catalina, it's not like that at all," Don exclaimed, stepping closer.

"We know they like you. If they were here with us, they would be just as aroused and wanton as we are."

"I'm sorry, Don. We can't make an assumption. Think about what you're saying to me. You're basically telling me that you and Cooper want to have an intimate relationship with me, a committed one, I hope, but that if your other two brothers are interested in sleeping with me to possibly see where it leads, I need to be willing and accepting of that? Do you realize how that sounds? I never even said yes to going out with you guys. I don't trust men for personal reasons, which I'm not getting into right now. I can't see what you're suggesting as anything but a disaster waiting to happen."

"Wait, I understand when you explain it like that. You're not a possession, a woman to fuck and be done with," Cooper told her, and she was astonished as her eyes widened and he gripped her hips. She held on to his forearms.

"Just focus on the two of us and what we feel right now. Let's see where it leads. If need be, Don and I decided that you come first, that you're so perfect for us, and we want this relationship."

"And if Jeremy and Cody come along, visit or whatever?" she asked, feeling a mix of anxiety, fear, and a bit of interest, which was truly strange. It was as though, in her mind, she thought she could accept them, too, but that kind of thinking would get her hurt.

Cooper cupped her cheeks between his hands. "We'll deal with it when and if the time comes. Just don't push us away." He leaned forward and kissed her deeply, pulling her completely into his embrace and making it so that the only thought in her mind when he lifted his lips from hers was whether or not Don would kiss her next.

Chapter 2

Jeremy walked out of the hardware store in town to find he had two flat tires. What the fuck were the chances of that happening? He cursed, knowing he had only the one spare in the back, and knew he would need a fucking tow. Great. His first week on leave from the job had given him nothing but time on his hands to sit and wonder what the fuck he wanted to do with his life. He was a goddamn trained killer, an agent for the government. In his ten years working numerous undercover operations, he'd pretended to be everything from a clerk who fronted a store for gun sales to a hired hit man working to eradicate the transmission of terrorist ideas onto the modern world.

He placed his hands on his hips and looked at the fucking tires. He pulled out his cell phone.

An hour later, he was sitting in the customer area of the local mechanic's shop waiting for the damn tires to be replaced. Finally, he handed over his credit card as the not-so-friendly cashier gave him some replies in a grunt and then handed over the card again.

As he pulled his car out of the gas station, he looked around the town. They were only about twenty-five minutes outside of Manhattan. He could get any open positions in another town, another city. As he thought about it, like he had been for the last several months, he came back to the same thing. He couldn't leave his brothers. It had been hell being away from them, and when they were all around, he felt at ease and at peace, but with Cooper and Don spending another week in Treasure Town, New Jersey, this was his week to straighten his shit out.

His cell phone rang, and he hit the speaker to answer it.

"Where ya at? You left early this morning," Cody said, sounding concerned.

"Fucking walked out of the hardware store to find two flat tires."

"Seriously?"

"Yep, then spent the last hour and a half sitting in the shop waiting for them to replace them."

"You're lucky you didn't take out the Mercedes."

"To go to the hardware store? No way. I should be back in about twenty minutes. What do you need?"

"It's not me who needs something. I just got back from taking a run. Don and Cooper need us to call them back. They have work in about an hour."

"Sounds like something is going on."

"Sure does. Cooper sounded serious."

"Shit. Was Don with him? Are they both okay?" he asked, but he knew they were. They had a special bond all these years, and despite being out of the loop for three years, his natural connection with them was getting stronger again. He would know if something was wrong.

"They're good. They swore they were."

"Okay, I'll see you soon."

The entire time he'd been home, Jeremy wondered what was up with his brothers. As he climbed the front porch to their large colonial, he saw some dirty boot marks, not remembering seeing them earlier when he left, but then he remembered he'd exited the house through the side door. When he got into the house, his stomach growled, and he realized he'd missed lunch and breakfast was a blur.

"Hey, what's up?" Cody asked as Jeremy entered the kitchen.

Jeremy walked over to the sink and washed his hands.

"Crazy fucking morning. Did the guys call back yet?"

"No. Any minute, though." Just then, the phone rang, and Cody answered it, putting it on speaker.

They exchanged pleasantries, and then Cooper cleared his throat.

"Don and I have been offered a really great job here in Treasure Town with the fire training center." Cooper went on about the job, the experience they'd had the last few weeks, and about wanting and needing a change in their lives. Jeremy felt his gut clench. One look at Cody and he knew his brother was feeling the same thing. They were drifting apart. All of them.

"That's a big decision to make in a matter of days, Cooper. Have you and Don thought this through?" But he knew in his heart they had thought it through. The twins always seemed to be able to make a decision on their own or together. Although mostly inseparable, they succeeded in all they did.

"There's more, guys. We're happy here. There are a lot of friends and a community that truly bonds together like nothing we've ever experienced before. We were hoping that the two of you would take the trip to come out here and see for yourself while you're both on leave from work. Maybe consider looking at what Treasure Town may have to offer you both."

Cody looked at Jeremy and shook his head.

"I don't know if I'm ready for that, to make a move like a career change or a different position than what I've been doing. I'll always wonder, you know, and if I hear of a situation, I'll think, what if I was involved?" Cody admitted.

"I feel the same way. I haven't decided what direction to go in yet. We don't want to lose you guys. We've always talked about living life together and handling things as a family." Jeremy felt his heart ache. He was causing this, all because he'd been removed from his position.

"There's more." Don said.

"Don, I thought we were going to wait," Cooper said to his brother. Jeremy and Cody could hear the whole conversation. They were on speaker.

"Shit. Hold on a minute. My cell is ringing. It's the chief," Don said, and they could hear the one-sided conversation. "Okay, fifteen minutes."

"We need to go, guys," Don said. "We'll call tomorrow and talk about this more. Think about coming out here for the upcoming weekend. We'd like to show you a few places we're looking at and think you'll both like."

"Yes, and with your professional experiences, there's certain to be something here for you as employment, whether in town or a short commute away. Call you tomorrow," Cooper said, and then they disconnected the call.

Jeremy gripped the table and exhaled. He slowly looked across the table at Cody.

"It is a great little town. We all loved it when we were there."

"I know we did, but if we decide to go check it out and consider giving up our old lives, do you think we'll be happy or wind up regretting it?"

"Jeremy, I don't know. Part of me is scared, but then when I think about my job and what I do, I know it's something I can do in any city or town. I stop terrorists from succeeding in causing deaths and damage. Treasure Town isn't that far from one of the larger headquarters for the anti-terrorist task force, but I don't know if I'm ready."

Jeremy exhaled and ran his hand along his jaw.

"I don't know if I'm ready either, but I was just getting used to having the three of you around me again. I missed three years of this, and I can't help but feel I'm to blame for causing us to lose that time. If I hadn't gone undercover—"

"No, Jeremy. That's not fair, and it's not the case at all. We've all chosen our careers. Hell, the dads even went through shit, too, when they met Mom."

"Shit, we're not even involved with a woman. What's supposed to come of that dream?"

Cody chuckled as he leaned back in the chair.

"I don't know. Maybe if we take Cooper and Don up on the offer to head out for the weekend to visit, we could get a date with that nurse we all met," Cody teased.

Jeremy chuckled.

"Catalina. Damn, she was gorgeous. I think we have too much shit to work out with ourselves before we could even think of asking a woman out. Hell, I didn't even know what I was doing for the rest of the night, never mind the next several years."

Cody stood up and walked to the refrigerator.

"Sounds like we need some beers."

He pulled two out as Jeremy chuckled, then sat back down at the table. Cody passed him a can of beer, and they both popped their cans open.

"To whatever tomorrow brings," Cody saluted.

"To whatever tomorrow brings," Jeremy repeated, and they clinked their cans of beer together and took a sip.

Hopefully it brings something positive.

* * * *

He listened as they spoke about their brothers and leaving for Treasure Town. He had been there just a few days ago watching the two other brothers. He knew their schedule, and he knew how he could take them out to get to Agent Jeremy Jones. His boss didn't want that quite yet. Instead, he wanted to play with Jeremy and get him to the point where his boss could use hurting the man's family as leverage when he confronted Jeremy and demanded information. Then he could point out how he could have just killed them and Jeremy if he wanted to.

It was Clover's job to keep watch, to do shit right under the agent's nose and, eventually, take what meant most to him away from him little by little. The dumbass was so out-of-sorts—and so was his brother Cody—that they didn't even seem suspicious of the car tires going flat. Nor did they sense the intrusion in their home as Clover bugged the place. He was good at what he did. Being patient and slowly torturing his victims was a specialty and a talent that would surely come in handy with one badass agent like Jeremy Jones.

He wrote down the information he needed, including the name of some woman they wanted to screw. It was all good stuff he would tell his boss about. He was going to love it when his boss revealed himself to Jeremy. Wouldn't that be a shocker? Everyone else thought he was dead or had long gone into hiding.

Not a man like Frederick Price. His friendship and business relationship with Castella Moya and Ruiz Mateo, who had been killed by Jeremy and some friends trying to save their woman Sophia, ran deep in their blood. Frederick wanted revenge, and so did Castella, but Agent Jones had information they could surely use to keep the illegal government business deals in motion. They just needed the names of other undercover agents, and Jeremy knew exactly who they were.

Clover couldn't wait. He'd tortured and killed so many agents before that getting this one, and his entire family if necessary, would be fun. They were the enemy and stood in the way of success and getting rich. For that alone, the Jones brothers all deserved to die.

* * * *

Cooper was across the walkway with a group of firefighters, training them on better procedures and safety measures while Don was having the firefighters do some physical conditioning and training to stay fit and increase their tolerance for high-cardio workouts. There were numerous stations set up, but the one that seemed to be gathering the most attention was a timed competition. They each had to carry over a hundred pounds of fire hose on their shoulder up ten flights of stairs and then use a fire extinguisher to put out a fire on the top floor.

Once the fire was out, they hooked up their ropes to descend down the side of the building and swing into the second floor, where they ran back up the staircase then down the side using the same ten flights they took to the top floor. As soon as they ran across the parking lot and past the orange cones, time was up. It was a very intense and difficult contest, and many of the firefighters failed to beat the top ten best times.

As Don stood by the next set of events, he chuckled as he heard four rookies getting ranked on by the more seasoned firefighters. They started talking trash, and then Cody heard a bunch of yelling and someone saying to "cool it" and "put that down." As Cody turned, he saw one rookie, who had been nothing but a wiseass from the start, swinging around his Halligan tool like some sword fighter. It was too late when he realized the kid had lost his grip. The tool went flying, hitting Don in the leg.

"What the fuck!" he roared as he grabbed his leg, the blood already seeping through his camo pocket pants.

"You stupid asshole. Get him the fuck out of here," one of the fire chiefs yelled as Cooper came running over, as did the other firefighters and their friends.

"Shit, Don," Ice said as he helped him to sit down. The guys were already over him, cutting his pants and looking at the damage to his leg.

"You need fucking stitches," Cooper said, but Don had known immediately he did.

"Fuck. What's wrong with those four fucking rookies? They think this is a goddamn joke? How the fuck did they pass the academy?" Don roared in anger, the pain now getting worse. His leg looked a mess.

"Let's apply pressure and wrap it up. We can get one of the guys over here with an ambulance. They're parked down the way," Bull said to him.

"Fuck that. Cooper will take me to the emergency room."

Cooper pointed at Ice and Bull. "You two take those fucking four asshole rookies and make them regret fooling around here. Tomorrow morning, I'm taking a look at their files and talking to the chiefs. I'm going to recommend they be re-evaluated and reinstated into the academy. The Halligan tool is not a fucking toy." Cooper then helped Don to get up.

Don couldn't believe this had happened, and at a fire training facility, no less. What the hell?

* * * *

Catalina was standing by the main desk when she got the call from Bull and Ice that Don had been hurt during training at the fire center. She was immediately concerned as he explained what had happened over the phone.

She got the attending physician to wait with her as Cooper and Don arrived. She could see the coloring in his face wasn't good. He was losing blood, and the shock of it all was hitting him.

"Lie down and relax, Don. This is Dr. Anders," Catalina told him as she placed her hand on his shoulder.

"Hey, Doc," Cooper said, but remained watching Catalina. She was so worried, she felt her heart racing. Even though it wasn't a life-threatening wound, Don would still need stitches.

"Hi, Catalina. I was hoping you would be here," Don admitted and gave her a wink.

She cleared her throat and looked at Dr. Anders, who smirked, and she tried to act professional.

"We missed you," Cooper said, flirting as the doctor looked at the damage and cleaned up the wound with Catalina's help.

She locked gazes with Don.

"There are better ways to visit then getting hit with a Halligan tool," she replied.

"How did you know it was a Halligan?" Don asked her.

"Bull and Ice called me and gave the heads-up."

Don smiled.

She shook her head at him and needed to remain professional here, despite how sexy and charming he looked. The fact that his friends had called her about the accident probably indicated to him that other people were thinking they were already in a relationship.

"We're still on for tonight, right, Catalina?" Don asked and looked at the doctor, who seemed surprised, and then got serious.

"I think you'll be in bed resting, Don. Just relax and we'll take care of everything," she reprimanded him, and Dr. Anders chuckled.

"You're going to need a good amount of stitches. If you'd been hit any harder, there would be serious tendon damage," the doctor told him.

"He jumped out of the way pretty quickly. He knows it could have been a lot worse, and we'll be taking care of those rookie firefighters tomorrow morning," Cooper told the doctor.

Catalina could see how angry Cooper was. She couldn't help but want to touch him, caress his arm, and give him a reassuring smile so he knew it was okay, but he just stared at Don as the doctor explained what he was going to do.

Dr. Anders asked her for several things, and when she got the tetanus shot, she reached out and held Don's arm.

"This might hurt a bit," Dr. Anders said to him, and Cooper cringed, but she felt Don's hand caress her outer thigh and then he didn't even flinch as the doctor injected the shot into the cut to ensure he didn't get an infection. She couldn't believe he didn't feel a thing. She held his gaze, his eyes completely focused on her.

"When do you get off work?" Don asked, and the doctor chuckled.

"When Dr. Anders says so." She turned toward the doctor and gathered the things needed to begin stitching up Don's leg.

"Cat, can you hold his thigh here so I can get these stitches nice and tight?" the doctor asked, and Catalina nodded and then ran her hand over Don's thigh and pressed where he told her.

"Sweet Jesus." Don exhaled, and she glanced at him and then at Cooper, who had his arms crossed and was chuckling.

As the doctor worked on the numerous stitches to Don's leg, she caught sight of something moving to the left and saw Bear and Ice peak around the large curtain separating them from the rest of the patients.

"Hey, you guys didn't have to come down," Cooper said, but then Jeremy and Cody walked in behind them, looking concerned.

"You guys had some visitors show up at the training facility. Thought we'd follow them over," Ice said and winked.

"Hey, Catalina. Got the best nurse in the place and the best doctor, huh?" Bear teased as he came next to the side of the bed and gave Don's shoulder a squeeze.

"Sure did," Don said and caressed Catalina's hip.

Catalina saw Cody's and Jeremy's expressions as they witnessed their brother caressing her hip, and she couldn't help but feel interested and excited. They were all here in one room. Jeremy and Cody were in town. What the hell was she going to do?

* * * *

Cody knew something was up. He couldn't take his eyes off of Catalina, and he saw the expression in Don's eyes as he caressed her hip and looked at Cody, then Jeremy. Catalina wasn't pulling away, and she looked a little flushed.

Jeremy moved closer and brushed by Catalina's side. Cody saw her expression and her cheeks turn a nice shade of pink.

"There we go. I'll just let Catalina clean this all up for you and then get everything you need," Dr. Anders said.

"We're going to head out. Take care of yourself and rest up tonight, Don. That was a good hit to the leg, and thirty stitches is a lot," Ice said and shook everyone's hand, along with Bear.

"Later, Cat," Bear said, and she waved.

They both exited the room, and then Cooper shook the doctor's hand as Dr. Anders brushed by Catalina, placing his hands on her hips to pass by her. Cody was instantly jealous.

As the doctor left the room, Cody and Jeremy greeted Cooper then Don.

"We meant to surprise you by showing up unannounced, but it seems you surprised us," Cody said to Cooper as he gave a hug and slap to Cooper's shoulder. They chuckled.

"This is fucking crazy, and all from some rookie firefighter?" Jeremy asked, but didn't take his eyes off Catalina.

"Yeah, well, it's over, and I'm fine, especially with my number-one nurse taking care of me. She was waiting on standby," he teased.

"You were there waiting for them? How did you know?" Jeremy asked her as he stepped closer.

"Ice called me. Let me finish this up and then get your release papers, Don, and also some instructions to follow to keep this clean."

Cooper took her hand to stop her.

"We're still on for tonight. Can't you help him with those instructions tonight?" Cooper asked and pulled her close.

"Cooper. I'm at work. We'll talk later."

"Okay. You remember my brothers, right?" he asked, holding her hand and then reaching up to caress her cheek.

She glanced at Cody and Jeremy. Cody looked her over in that nurse's uniform and white medical coat she had on. She looked so sexy.

"Of course I do."

"Good. I'll pick you up at your place around seven." He leaned forward and kissed her lips.

Cody felt his cock harden and couldn't take his eyes off of Catalina. He could feel the sexual chemistry in the room. He had a bunch of questions for his brothers. Holy crap, he couldn't believe how affected he was at seeing her. Was she seeing Cooper and Don, and for how long?

Were they seeing her? How long had they been? Why hadn't they told him and Jeremy? Did this have to do with why they'd asked him and Jeremy to visit? Would she be interested in all of them? Were they sleeping with her?

His expression must have been super serious, and the same with Jeremy, because as Catalina stepped away and headed toward the door, she looked scared.

The second the curtain closed, Jeremy spoke before Cody had a chance to.

"What the hell is going on? You're seeing her?" Jeremy asked.

Cooper smiled as he leaned against the examining table where Cody still lay waiting. He smiled, too.

"We just started seeing her," Cooper told them.

"Is it serious?" Cody asked, moving closer and watching his brothers.

"We're going to take that new job. Does that answer your question?" Don asked.

Cody swallowed hard. Why hadn't they told them over the phone? Did they want to share her or keep her for themselves, and why did that question make him feel sick and utterly disappointed?

The curtain to the bay opened and in came Catalina. She was carrying some papers and a pen. She avoided eye contact with Cody and Jeremy and went to Don.

"Okay, Dr. Anders said you need to follow these instructions to the T, or else. Just sign here and I can get things moving quickly so you can head home to rest."

Don signed the papers. "Not rest entirely. You're coming over for dinner."

She glanced around the bay.

"We can do that another time. Your brothers came into town to surprise you."

"It appears we're the ones who are surprised. You three get together, and we'll fend for ourselves tonight," Jeremy said.

"Don't be ridiculous. You come over to our place and stay with us. We rented a house a few blocks from the beach. There's plenty of room for all of us," Cooper stated.

"All of us?" Cody asked and eyed over Catalina.

"Definitely," Don replied and then handed her the paperwork.

She placed the documents down on the small table and then handed Don's copies to Cooper. She started to help Don to sit up, and he totally took advantage of the opportunity to grab onto her. She caressed his shoulder, and Cody watched how sincere and caring she was, as Don looked a little peaky.

"That dizziness will pass."

She caressed his cheek, and he turned his face and kissed her palm.

"I may need a bedside nurse tonight, Catalina."

She chuckled as she placed her hands on his hips and held his gaze.

"You'll need those painkillers and lots of rest."

"I'm fine, baby. I was looking forward to seeing you all day today."

She smiled at him. "Then let me wrap things up here. I'll see you later."

"I'll pick you up at seven," Cooper stated firmly, and she nodded and headed out of the room.

* * * *

They all sat in the living room with Don as he lay on the couch.

"So you saw her at the Station and started talking to her, and then ask her to come home with you?" Jeremy repeated and shook his head. He wanted to know all the details. His brothers looked so happy.

"It was an intense moment, man. She looked so sexy and beautiful. I was overwhelmed with emotions and feeling so damn possessive. Man, even that day Don and I were headed to Sullivan's and these guys were bothering her, I was so ready to tear them limb from limb."

"Me too," Don added.

"Did they try to hurt her?" Jeremy asked, sitting forward in his seat.

"No, we got to her in time. It just pissed us the hell off. But then we had lunch, and we talked and made some plans. We only went out one other time, and again, it wasn't planned. She had just finished her shift at work, and I was walking down the boardwalk, getting ready to meet Don. We bumped into her again and grabbed dinner. Ate on the boardwalk by the park."

Jeremy glanced at Cody, who sipped a bottle of Bud.

"We're happy for you guys," he said, but felt his tone weaken.

"We're glad, but this is just the beginning," Cooper told him. "We were kind of hoping that you both felt the same attraction to Catalina. It's why we called and told you about the job offer, and to consider moving here. We're tired of the way things were. Treasure Town is an amazing town filled with great people. You two would love it here. Maybe consider staying here with us. We're supposed to look at some houses for sale this Sunday."

Jeremy exhaled as he stood up. He paced half the room.

"Did you even discuss this with Catalina? I mean, she met the two of you, has an attraction to the both of you, but you can't force this kind of relationship, Coop."

"Don't you think we know that? We talked to her about it in the beginning. Her fear is that she doesn't want to be a possession, an item."

"That's understandable, but is she even interested in a ménage relationship with four men?" Cody asked.

"She's not dead set against it. Her friends are involved in them. We said we'd take things slow, and we have," Cooper stated and looked at Don.

"You sleep with her yet?" Jeremy asked.

"No. It's new. Your timing is perfect, Jeremy. She could be the woman we've been waiting for, the one that completes this family," Cooper said to him.

"But Cody and I don't know what we're doing about work yet. It wouldn't be fair to try and have a long-distance relationship until we can figure shit out. It is bad timing," he said, feeling insecure about the whole thing and not even knowing if Catalina was attracted to him and Cody, too.

"Let's just see how tonight goes. She's really sweet and a damn good kisser," Don stated and leaned back, placing his arms behind his head as he exhaled.

"And she'll probably cater to you all night as you pretend to be some invalid," Cooper said and threw a pillow at his brother's head.

"Hey. I could have lost my fucking leg."

"But you didn't."

Jeremy and Cody laughed.

"I'm going to go pick up Catalina. One of you want to come with me?" Cooper asked Jeremy and Cody."

"You think that's a good idea?" Cody asked.

"If she's going to get used to all of us as a package deal and get to know you then, yes, it's a good idea," Cooper said.

"You go, Jeremy. I'll sit here with Don," Cody said.

"No, you go. Don and Coop stink at cooking. I can get the potatoes ready and sauté the vegetables while Don takes a little nap," he teased, and they chuckled.

Cody stood up and wiped his hands on his jeans. "I'll be right back," he said and exited the room.

Jeremy looked at Cooper.

"I don't want to ruin this for you guys. I'm really not in the right frame of mind. I know we talked about being a family, following our parents' tradition, but things have changed so much. I don't even know what I want to do with my life. I'm not even sure I know if I can do anything different from being an undercover agent. I just feel out-of-sorts right now."

"It's understandable, and there's no pressure here. All we ask is that you're honest about what you feel and, if you're attracted to Catalina, that you take your time and you don't fake anything. Don and I feel she's the one. If you and Cody can't love her and don't feel it like we do, then don't lie or pretend. Just move on because we'll always be your brothers, no matter what."

Jeremy nodded as Cody came out smiling.

"All good, Romeo?" Cooper teased.

"Well, you had a first date with her. I don't want to come across as an escort or third wheel, okay?"

"So you want to kill her with cologne?" Cooper teased and waved his hand in front of his nose as if trying to get rid of the smell of men's cologne.

"No, I want her to win her heart with my sexy, masculine ways. You're just jealous because I'm bigger," Cody told Cooper and Jeremy, and Don chuckled.

"Your head is bigger, that's for sure. Let's go."

"My head is bigger than all of yours, and not the one on my shoulders. Peace out, Don, Jeremy. We'll be back with something sweet and sexy. Start cooking dinner," Cody teased. Jeremy shook his head and Cooper chuckled.

"Oh God, he is going to embarrass us tonight."

* * * *

"Will you calm down? This is what you've been waiting for. To find some men of your own you can fall in love with and be a part of," Serefina told Catalina as they spoke on the phone.

"It's not the same like this. I met and talked with Don and Cooper first."

"And you discussed the possibility that their brothers might come around and be interested, too, but that they're going through some stuff."

"I don't want to be a sex toy for them to play with whenever they have the urge to share a woman."

"Oh, come on. They're not like that at all. They said their parents are in a ménage relationship. They know how this works. I'm sure they're just worried because of what happened with Jeremy and his job when Sophia was abducted. He lost a lot. He has to decide what type of job to do now. It's overwhelming and stressful. Plus, Cody isn't sure what he's doing. So there are things to work out. Just take your time and go slow, but follow your heart, Catalina. It will be fine."

"I believe you're right, I do, but I'm sort of insecure still. I've never had a meaningful relationship. I had sex because it was the next step, and then realized I made a mistake. Intimacy scares me. I've spent so much time alone and focusing on work I don't know how to let go and just have fun and enjoy life."

"Then all of this is actually good timing. The new job offer, meeting Cooper and Don, and now their brothers, too. It's meant to be, Catalina. Now is the time to take some chances since you've been playing it safe for so long."

"But I can't help but think about Paul and college."

"That's understandable, but I remember when all that bad shit went down. You didn't think you could ever trust or love a man again. Now look at you. You're stronger, more mature, and you're not afraid to put on the brakes or question integrity. I say be honest with them. Take your time and see what happens tonight."

Catalina looked in the mirror. She ran her hands down the strapless sundress she wore. It hugged her curves and ended right above her knees. Her legs looked great with the high-heeled sandals, too. Then she heard the doorbell ring.

"I need to go."

"I heard. Good luck and be safe. If they hurt you, my men will kick their asses."

Catalina chuckled, and then hurried out of her bedroom and down the small hallway to the living room. Her townhouse had two bedrooms and was perfect for just her.

She took a deep breath and opened the front door. She was shocked to see Cody with Cooper.

"You look gorgeous, baby." He stepped closer, wrapped his arms around her waist, and kissed her softly on the cheek. She held on to his forearms and smiled.

"Thank you. So do you guys," she said as he gently released her and stepped back.

"Catalina," Cody said and reached his hand out to her.

She placed her hand into his. "Cody," she whispered, and when he brought her hand to his lips and kissed the top of it, she felt the butterflies in her belly. *God, he's so good-looking. They both are.*

"This is a nice place," Cody said as he released her hand and stepped inside. Cooper closed the door and looked around.

"Thank you. I've lived here for several years now. It's a nice complex and only a few blocks from the beach."

"That's not a long drive at all," Cody told her.

"I either bike or run, so I don't mind at all."

"You run a lot?" Cody asked her.

"Yes, it's my favorite form of exercise."

"Do any marathons or races?" he asked her.

"Actually, a few, but I'm considering a longer one."

"Really? Is there one coming up around here?" Cody asked.

"There's some 10K race in another week or so. I think a fundraising event for charity," Cooper said, adding to the conversation.

"Ten K, huh? Sounds like fun."

"Do you like to run?" she asked Cody.

"I do, but I haven't done a race in a while."

"I've been trying to train with some of my friends, but I'm not quite happy with my times."

"How often do you run?" Cody asked.

"With work, I try to go at least four times a week, but I tend to lose a couple of days when I transition from night shift to day shift. In fact, I need to run tomorrow. I'm up to fourteen miles."

"Damn, that's impressive," Cooper told her, and she smiled.

"So are you all set?" Cooper asked.

"Definitely. How is Don feeling? Is he in a lot of pain?" she asked as they walked out the door and she locked up. Cooper led the way, and Cody followed behind her.

"He'll be fine. He's had worse injuries. I think he's just pissed off at the rookie who caused it," Cooper told her over his shoulder.

"Well, he should be. What the hell was he thinking, swinging around a Halligan tool like that?"

She gasped as they got to the sidewalk and Cooper stopped short as some kids sped by on bikes, yelling "sorry" as they passed. She felt Cody press up against her as he bumped into her from behind, and he wrapped an arm around her waist.

"Okay, beautiful?" he asked, and as she tilted her head back to look at him, he kissed her bare shoulder. She nodded as her nipples hardened and her heart began to pound.

"All safe now," Cooper told her.

She turned, and they headed toward the truck together with Cody still keeping a hand on her hip. She loved the scent of his cologne. It smelled familiar, and as they paused by the truck and Cody opened the passenger door, she turned to look at him.

"What cologne is that you're wearing?" she asked.

Cooper hopped into the truck on the other side. "You mean the one he doused himself in?" he teased.

"You like it?" Cody asked and looked down into her eyes, holding her gaze.

He looked a lot like Don and Cooper, but his dark hair was crew-cut. He wore a thin gold chain, and his lips looked firm but tender.

"I do. It smells familiar."

"Remind you of someone else?" he asked and pressed closer to her.

He moved her hair off her shoulder and lowered his mouth to her neck, allowing her nostrils to fill with his scent and also feel his masculine touch. She inhaled. "Like Don. You both use the same one?" she whispered, and when he pulled slowly back, his lips were inches from hers. All she had to do was move toward him, but would it be right? Was she playing with fire?

Cody made the decision for her.

"You smell so good, too, Catalina. I wonder how you taste."

He then pressed his lips softly to hers. She felt his arm go around her waist, and then his lips deepened the kiss before he slowly pulled back. He took an unsteady breath along with her.

"My God, you're so special. Come on, the others are probably getting impatient to see you."

She slowly turned, and when she went to step onto the side rail to get into the truck, Cody lifted her up and placed her gently onto the seat with ease. He slid in next to her and smiled at her, then Cooper.

Cooper ran his hand along her thigh and gave it a squeeze.

"All set, baby?"

She nodded and prayed she wasn't making the biggest mistake of her life.

* * * *

Jeremy watched Catalina take care of Don. In fact, he hadn't been able to take his eyes off of Catalina since she'd arrived over an hour ago. She was stunning, and all three of his brothers fell into a natural comfort zone with her. When he wasn't trying so hard to keep his distance, he found himself trying to step closer to her. To rub by her, to inhale her perfume, and to feel the magnetic tug at his body making him want to touch her.

But could he give her what she deserved, what his brothers deserved, or was he so unsure of what he wanted and too obsessed with what he thought he had to be in life? Tonight was bringing him closer to figuring it out but also deeper into wanting the things they had all talked about more than five years ago.

* * * *

"This was so good. Who made the potato salad?" Catalina asked as she took one more forkful. She was pretty hungry, but was relieved to have a home-cooked meal instead of trying to scrape something up at home for just her.

"You can thank Jeremy. He's a wiz in the kitchen," Cooper told her.

"Actually, we're all more than capable of cooking. Our mother and fathers made certain of that," Don told her, and then he sat back and exhaled.

She could see the perspiration reach his brow. He was tired and trying to stay up and enjoy the evening, but getting stitches could be exhausting. Plus, he was still so angry at the rookie firefighters. It seemed to have taken its toll.

"You should see the things Jeremy has been whipping up in the kitchen lately. I think he found his second calling," Cody teased, and Jeremy gave him a sideways glance.

"Really? Well. I expect to benefit from this new hobby of yours, bro. You know I have a huge appetite," Cooper said as he rubbed his belly, but then he looked at Catalina. His eyes roamed over her breasts and then to her lips, and she shyly turned away.

They were too much, each of them flirting every chance they got.

"So, have you decided to apply for that position at the hospital or what, Catalina?" Don asked her, and she could see the strain on his face. He really was fighting the pain he was in. He probably didn't want his brothers or her to see him weak, but his body had gone through something traumatic. Even though it wasn't a super-deep cut, he had still needed stitches. She reached over and caressed his hand.

"I'm leaning closer toward applying. I heard from one of the supervisors on the board, and word spread quickly that I'm the only one in the hospital now that has the credentials and experience."

"You sound a little unsure. What's holding you back?" Jeremy asked, leaning forward in his chair.

She took a deep breath and exhaled.

"I love working in the ER and being there when things happen. I feel like I can truly be beneficial to patients and the doctors during some of the most intense moments."

"Would this position not allow for you to still assist?" Cody asked her.

"Well, technically, I would be spending less time in the ER hands-on as a nurse and half the time doing some administrative work, like dealing with grants, bringing funding to the different departments in need. But the position is new, and there aren't specific guidelines, and it seems to involve a lot of responsibilities. It's like being the head nurse of the ER. In our hospital, the position only allows eight-to-ten-hour shifts, but also doing administrative work. The hours don't seem right. Right now, they're only in need of the days, so I would work a normal eight-to-four shift. I just don't know if I would be happy."

"Well, not working crazy hours or nights sounds like a ideal position, especially when you not only get to do a job you love but also remain with the staff who knows you and more than likely respects you already," Jeremy told her.

"I'm so used the chaos of the night shifts, too, but I'm tired of this pasty night-shift coloring I have." She ran her hands along her arms.

"You look pretty damn beautiful to me," Cooper told her from across the table.

She felt her cheeks blush and cleared her throat.

"What about you and Cody? Any ideas what you want to do, or are you guys considering different positions in the agencies you work for now?" she asked.

"I guess I'm kind of feeling like you are, Catalina. Like if I leave, something might go down where, if I had been there, it could have made a difference. It's the not knowing," Cody admitted.

"That's understandable, but sometimes change is good and things happen for a reason. I was pretty close to moving out of town completely," she admitted.

"Really? Why?" Jeremy asked her.

"I thought there was nothing more for me to achieve here in Treasure Town, and to be honest, I'm seeing all these changes around me with a lot of my friends, and I started wondering if I could be stuck in a rut. Five years have gone by so quickly. Five more and I'll be thirty and trying to decide on a retirement plan, or maybe I might be burned out by then, because a lot of ER nurses do get burned out. I could miss this opportunity and great pay for this new position. It's so stressful and emotional at times, and you have to keep it together. It takes a toll."

"I think that's what Cody and I are feeling, too. Like we could get burnt out, or we're in a rut and need something new, yet what we do is our calling, so how do we give it up?" Jeremy asked.

"Maybe we don't give it up. Maybe we try to find something similar but with less danger, stress, or the things that we can identify as stuff that could burn us out. I don't know. I guess life is about taking chances, and this is one I'm going to have to face and just decide already," Cody said.

"Us too," Cooper added.

"If that position you mentioned is new, can the responsibilities be altered or better clarified to your specific interests, capabilities, and experience? Maybe discussing that possibility with your boss might help clarify things and direct you toward making the right decision?" Jeremy suggested.

She stared at him, in awe of his idea. The fact that she'd sat here talking to the four of them for hours now was unreal. She could get used to this, to having them around to bounce ideas off of and to have their support, but Cody and Jeremy were still unsure where they were headed. Did it even matter to her? She felt so attracted to them, especially now as all four added their comments and their support to her.

She smiled and then looked at Don as he gave her a wink but cringed.

"You aren't feeling well, are you?" she asked.

She stood up and placed her hand on his shoulder. She reached for his napkin and wiped his brow. "What you went through was traumatic for your body. Sometimes you need to listen to it and take a rest. You should take some painkillers and lie down."

He gripped her wrist and brought it to his lips, kissing the inside of it. She held his gaze. His other arm wrapped around her waist and pulled her close. She nearly wound up on his lap.

"Don, I'll hurt you."

"Never," he whispered and kissed farther along her arm from wrist to elbow.

"Don."

"Help me out here, Catalina." He pressed her thigh against him and then lowered his good leg so she had to straddle it. He pulled her by her ass up onto his thigh, and she gasped and grabbed onto his shoulder.

"Kiss me, Catalina," Don told her.

It was odd, but she was entirely turned on by his masculinity and his move to get her this close. She worried about his injured leg while she straddled his good one, but she wasn't worried about the audience.

He released her wrist, and she ran her hands along his chest and shoulders as she stared down into his gorgeous eyes. The feel of both his hands massaging her thighs and then moving under her dress had her shaking with need. His hands massaged her ass cheeks. She pressed her lips gently to his and then pulled back.

"More," he whispered, giving her thighs a squeeze.

She ran her fingers through his hair and caressed his cheeks as she kissed Don deeply. His hands held firm, and he kissed her back, deepening the kiss, plunging his tongue into her mouth in exploration. She felt hot, on fire, as she moved closer. When his hand reached under her dress again and cupped her ass cheeks, massaging them, pressing them apart and then together, she moaned into his mouth. He pulled her back and forth as she rocked her hips until she felt his finger glide into the crack of her ass against her anus.

"Don," she gasped after pulling from his mouth.

It was so wild, and her mind erupted in crazy, sexy thoughts of being with all these men and having them touch her intimately, making love to her together and filling every hole. She gripped Don's shoulders and caught her breath.

"I want to feel how wet you are. I want to taste you." He pulled her higher up, parting her thighs and stroking her crack.

"So do we," Cooper said, and she swung her head around to see Cooper, Cody, and Jeremy watching her with hunger in their eyes.

"I thought we were going to take this slow?" she asked, breathless.

"Slow is overrated," Don said and pulled her down for a kiss.

He explored her mouth with his tongue, and she could hear the dishes moving, chairs scraping against the floor, and then she felt the second set of hands on her shoulders from behind. She wasn't sure who joined them until Cooper spoke.

"Let us pleasure you, baby, and get to know this body. We'll only go as far as you want," he whispered and kissed her bare shoulder.

Don stopped kissing her.

"Help her onto the table. It's the perfect height for me to taste her sweet cream," Don said to Cooper as he began to lift her up.

"Don. Oh God, I don't know about this." But as she said the words, Cooper lifted her up with Don's help and gently laid her on the kitchen table. Don pressed her dress upward and caressed her legs from ankle to thighs. When he got to her hips, he held her gaze.

"Lift up."

As he removed her panties, she shivered and shook, felt her pussy leak with anticipation of his touch, and Don smiled.

"This is what I really need. You're my medicine, baby. Every gorgeous inch of you." He leaned forward, cringed a little from his obvious pain from his leg, and then stroked a finger along her pussy lips. He used his thumb to spread her cream and cause little vibrations to fill her pussy. Then she felt his mouth on her inner thigh, sucking, pulling, leaving love bites on his pathway to her cunt.

Cooper leaned over the table and cupped her cheeks.

"You're more than we could have hoped for. Your body is perfection."

He kissed her deeply just as Don pressed his tongue to her pussy and began to feast. It was sensation overload when she gasped and lifted her hips, then felt her top being pressed down and her breasts exposed. Cody joined in the fun and began to lick her nipples and then suckle her breasts with his hot, wet mouth. Her belly tightened, and she felt Don switch from tongue to two fingers, eliciting another moan from her.

Cooper released her lips and began to feast on her breasts.

"Holy fuck, you're gorgeous, Catalina. I want to taste you, too," Jeremy said, and the look in his eyes was so dark, so deep, she felt a shiver run through her system. He leaned forward from behind her, traced gently along her jaw as he held her gaze. It was a strong contrast to the deep, hard sucks on her breasts from Cooper and Cody, as well as the hard, fast strokes from Don. She felt so alive, so desirable it had her shaking with need for more, but as Jeremy gently cupped her face and kissed her from above, suckling her lower lip into his mouth, nibbling on her chin and then plunging his tongue into her mouth, the sensations overwhelmed her system. She felt her body explode as the orgasm rocked her from head to toe.

"I need a taste," Cooper said as he released her breast.

Like some sort of assembly line, they rotated. Jeremy kept kissing her. Cody moved into Don's position, and Cooper helped Cody.

She moaned into Jeremy's mouth, and he just kept kissing her and then ran his hands along her shoulder to her breast, cupping it. She ran her hands through his hair and held him to her breast as she tilted her head back and let go, relishing the effects on her body.

A moment later she felt Cody's fingers thrust up into her cunt. Thick, hard, and long, his finger stroked her, hitting a sensitive spot that made her pussy spasm some more.

"So fucking wet and tight. Damn, baby, you are perfect and so giving," Cody said while he thrust his fingers and then licked along her lips.

He alternated tongue and fingers, and she moaned again and lifted her hips upward. Jeremy released her lips and moved along to the side, where he cupped her breast and then began to feast on her breast, tugging on her nipple.

Cooper was back exploring her other breast and nipple, and then Cody's mouth suckled hard on her pussy, eliciting a squeal from her throat, and she came again.

He slurped and licked, cleaning her up, and then lifted up, smiling. "Fucking delicious."

She turned away, feeling embarrassed and turned-on, and she locked gazes with Don. He sat in the chair right to the side, his pants unzipped and his cock in his hand. Their gazes locked, and he looked so carnal and needy. She wanted to go to him and ease that ache, but then Cody was moving and Cooper was taking his place. There was no preamble, just fingers thrusting into her cunt and Cooper's lips, tongue, and teeth feasting on her pussy lips and then her anus. She nearly shot off the table when he touched her there, but Jeremy held down her shoulder and gripped her chin.

"What's my brother doing to you, baby?"

"Oh God, this is wild. Too much." She moaned as Cooper suckled her pussy with his mouth, and then she would feel his tongue roll between her pussy lips and over her anus. Back and forth, every stroke made her feel so needy and aroused.

"Oh God. Oh, Cooper."

"What is he doing? Tell me," Jeremy demanded, and she felt her pussy cream.

"Fuck, I think she likes your tone, Jeremy. She's leaking like a fucking faucet," Cooper said and then licked again.

Jeremy held her gaze and leaned down closer.

"Where is his tongue stroking?"

She felt her chest tighten, and she knew she loved this. She was turned on by his demanding tone, his big muscles, and his need to hear the dirty talk.

"My pussy," she whispered, and Cooper slowly pressed a finger to her anus.

She thrust upward.

"And?" Cooper pushed.

"My ass. Oh God I never…" She moaned, and then she shook as she came.

She was panting for breath as Jeremy held her gaze.

"Ever been with more than one man?"

She shook her head fast.

"Ever have a cock in your ass?" he asked, and she shook her head fast again.

"That's fucking hot. We're going to be your firsts, aren't we, Catalina? You want us to be your firsts? You want me to fuck this ass while Cooper fucks that pussy and Don strokes his cock into your sweet, sexy mouth?"

"Oh God!" She screamed another release.

"And then I get to make love to you last. Just when you think you can't go anymore, I'll give you another orgasm," Cody told her as he leaned down and nibbled her shoulder.

Jeremy moved around her, and Cooper moved from between her legs but kissed her on the mouth. She could taste her cream on his lips and then his tongue as he plunged it into her mouth. She reached up and grabbed hold of him, feeling so overwhelmed, but then he pulled back and Jeremy was there to take his place. Jeremy lifted her thighs over his shoulders as he sat in the chair in front of the table with her ass and pussy in his face.

He closed his eyes and inhaled.

"Fuck, you smell as sweet as honey."

He swiped his tongue over her pussy all the way to her anus. Back and forth, he licked her as he massaged her inner thighs. She reached down and held on to his head, tilted her head back, and enjoyed his tactics while moaning and panting for breath. A nip from his teeth then a suckle against a more sensitive spot had her wriggling on the table and moving her head side to side.

When one finger entered her ass and another entered her pussy and began a series of strokes, she cried out another release, but Cooper and Cody were there to hold her arms above her head and then explore her breasts. She was restrained by three men while the fourth one stroked his cock, and he was so turned-on that she wanted to come. She wanted to let them fuck her. She never felt so wild and aroused in her life, and nothing had ever felt so right.

Jeremy kissed along her thighs and then lowered her legs back down, easing his fingers from both holes. He eased his way over her body. Cooper and Cody still held her arms above her head, and her breasts were fully exposed. Jeremy licked along one breast and tugged, then licked along the other and tugged, holding her gaze with a dark, determined look.

"You were made for us, Catalina. I believe that, but going slow just may not be an option tonight." He covered her mouth and kissed her.

Cody and Cooper kissed along her arms and then released them. She hugged Jeremy tight and wrapped her legs around his thighs, and he lifted her up and began to carry her out of the kitchen.

When he set her feet down on the floor and placed his hands against the zipper of her dress as he stared into her eyes, she knew she wanted to be with them.

"Stay with us tonight. Make love to us."

"This is so crazy. I hardly know you."

"You know enough. You know what we want, what we expect from this, and I think you want that, too."

"You aren't even sure you know what you want to do with your lives. A long-distance relationship might not work."

"That may be true, but feeling you, being with you tonight, has made things clearer. It will take time to work things out, but I know I want you. My brothers do, too, and that's something we've always dreamed about. We waited for you, Catalina, and the timing has to be right. It has to be," Jeremy told her.

He caressed her back, his large, firm hands over her skin arousing her senses. She felt so in tune to each of these men. She wanted to be loved, cared for, and to have a real relationship with honest, good men. Was it the right time to take this chance?

He pressed closer and began to play with the zipper on the back of her dress. Cooper moved in behind her and kissed her shoulder.

"We won't hurt you."

"I must be out of my mind," she whispered and then pressed her hands against Jeremy's chest and ran them up along his shirt to his shoulders. As he leaned down to meet her lips with his, she felt the zipper go down on her dress, and it fell to the floor.

"Sweet mercy, woman, you have one hell of an ass," Cody told her, and Don chuckled.

"One hell of a body, bro," Don said as Jeremy continued to kiss her.

She had to admit that, despite her hard workouts and being so health-conscious, she worried about how her body might look to them. She had been alone for so long, not ever trusting any men, never mind four, enough to be intimate and have sex with them. She was fully exposing herself to these four men in every way. Her body, her heart, and her soul were all on the table. Would she get hurt? God, she prayed not. How could this be wrong and feel so good, so right as each of them touched her.

Jeremy moved his lips from hers to her jaw and to her neck. Behind her, Cooper lowered, and she felt his fingers spread her ass cheeks as his tongue located her slit.

"I'm going to need some serious creative tactics here, guys," Don said as he sat on the edge of the bed completely naked, his leg all bandaged up as he stroked his cock.

Jeremy cupped her breast as he lowered his mouth to her nipple and tugged.

Cody joined in on the other side, taking her breast into his mouth and licking her areola before suckling the tiny, hard bud between his teeth. Sensations traveled through a string of nerves from her nipples to her pussy, making her moan and come a little.

"Let me," she said as Jeremy and Cody released her breasts.

Cooper followed her as she turned to the left and lowered to her knees in front of Don. She ran her hands up his thighs, being careful to avoid the bandage and the side of his leg where the stitches were. He ran his hands through her hair.

"I'm going to beat the crap out of that fucking rookie first chance I fucking get." He looked so angry and serious that she knew she needed to calm him down. They could do this. They could all make love tonight.

She leaned forward and licked the tip of his cock. Don hissed.

"Just relax and let me take care of you," she told him as she looked up into his eyes

"Goddamn," Cooper whispered and stepped in behind her.

He lowered to his knees and ran his hands along her legs from ankles to thighs and hips. Then he spread her thighs wider and pulled her hips back. She inhaled at the way Cooper parted her thighs and then placed a hand on her hip to squeeze her closer while he found her clit with his other finger and began to stimulate her cunt. Don gripped her hair and slowly stroked into her mouth, and that was it. She opened for him, wanting to please him, to make him come in her mouth since he might not be able to come inside of her body.

The connection, the deep, instant need to please, to want to protect and care for him, for them, was overwhelming. So as Cooper maneuvered his fingers into her cunt from behind and started to stroke faster and faster, she thrust her hips back and relished his capabilities and this moment. Tomorrow would be a different story entirely.

* * * *

"You're so giving, Catalina. You want to please us, don't you, baby?" Jeremy asked, taking a seat on the bed.

He was naked and his cock so hard and needy to be inside of Catalina. He caressed her shoulder and stroked a finger along her cheek as she sucked on Don's cock. Don had his eyes closed, and behind Catalina, Cooper smiled. Jeremy watched Cooper press over her much-smaller frame as he stroked her pussy, making her thrust back against Cooper's fingers. Jeremy felt his cock grow harder at the way Cooper licked her skin and then moved his hand over her waist to the front of her.

"Open for me. Offer me this sweet pussy, baby."

"Oh hell, Coop," Don complained, and his face contorted as he seemed to be trying to hold his ground and not come in Catalina's mouth.

Jeremy gripped her hair. "Cody, grab the lube and the condoms."

Catalina gasped but kept sucking on Don's cock as Cooper switched hands and maneuvered the one in the front of her to stroke fingers up into her cunt. Cody appeared with the tube of lube and two boxes of condoms.

"Feeling that sure of yourself?" Jeremy teased.

"Fuck yeah. I want in every hole. I want to mark her as our woman and make her see that there'll never be another man but the four of us," Cody said and then tossed the condoms on the bed.

"Oh, damn. Damn, Coop, what are you doing to her?" Don asked and started panting then thrusting his hips faster.

Catalina was sucking and moving her head up and down. One look over her shoulder and Jeremy could see Cooper's other fingers pressing the lube in her ass, spreading her and getting her ready for their cocks.

"I need you, baby. Say you want us," Cooper said, pulling his fingers from her body. She nodded, and he smoothed his hands along her ass, squeezing her ass cheeks.

"Cody?" Cooper said, and Cody handed him a condom. A moment later, Cooper was gripping Catalina's hips.

"Here I come, baby. Time to make you all ours."

Jeremy caressed her back just as Cooper stroked his cock into her pussy from behind. When Catalina began to push back, Jeremy knew that this was going to be a wild night. She wanted them. They wanted her, and nothing had ever come even remotely close to this sensation.

"Fuck, I'm there. I can't hold back. Fuck," Don yelled out and then shot his load into Catalina's mouth. She sucked and caressed him, and then he pulled from her mouth and she kissed his inner thighs.

"Catalina?" Jeremy whispered to her and caressed her cheek. She looked at him, her lips wet, parted, and her cheeks rosy pink. She was gasping and moaning as Cooper thrust into her pussy harder, faster.

"Oh God. Oh, Cooper," she moaned.

Jeremy was shocked when Catalina pushed back and then moved in between Jeremy's legs to cup his cock and balls. She ran her hands along his inner thighs and stroked his muscle.

"Holy hell, woman. God, those hands feel so good, but I'm going to be inside of you when I come. You hear me, baby? Inside of that sexy ass."

He stroked her hair, and Cooper slowed his pace behind her. Jeremy locked gazes with him.

Cooper's expression was so intense and filled with such emotion. Jeremy glanced at Cody, who moved closer.

"Together. Let's take her together and make this official."

Cooper eased his cock from her pussy, and Catalina released Jeremy's cock.

She was breathing erratically, her chest all patchy with red marks, her breasts full and perfect.

"We want you together. We'll go slow, baby. We all need to take you tonight."

Cooper gave her hips a tap. He then lay down on the bed with his legs hanging off the bed as Jeremy stood up. Cooper curled his finger at her, indicating for her climb up on top of him.

Jeremy helped her up, feeling her sexy body and how light and feminine she was. He suddenly had such a possessive feeling come over him. He felt protective of her, and he knew that protectiveness would get stronger.

She slid down over Cooper's cock, taking it up into her cunt slowly as she eased up and down. She ran her hands along his chest as Jeremy took the lube from Cody and squirted some to her ass as he pressed a finger against her puckered hole.

"Oh God. It burns, Jeremy. It feels so odd."

"Just relax those muscles. Let us in, Catalina," Cody whispered to her and leaned forward to kiss her shoulder, and then down her upper arm to her exposed breast.

He suckled and feasted on her as Cooper gripped her hips and pressed upward while Jeremy maneuvered his fingers faster, deeper into her ass. He scissored his fingers, stretching her inner muscles, preparing her for his cock. He felt the pre-cum drip from the tip of his cock and prayed he would last more than a few strokes, but she was incredibly aroused, and she was absolutely perfect in every way. She was their woman. There was no doubt in his mind.

"I'm coming in next, baby. Get ready for Cody, too, now," Jeremy instructed. Being in charge, leading this lovemaking session and taking care of his family was his job, his calling. The fact that he immediately thought of Catalina as family struck his heart as he thrust his fingers a little faster. Catalina moaned and thrust back against his digits. She was super wet when Cody tilted her head toward his cock and then pressed it between her lips. She explored Cody's cock with her mouth and tongue and then accepted his strokes, tilting her head back and accommodating his thick, hard cock.

"Here I come."

Jeremy eased his fingers from her ass and replaced them with the tip of his cock.

"Goddamn, this is fucking wild and sexy as damn hell," Don said from the bed. He was sitting up watching, stroking his cock again.

Jeremy chuckled, but then he clenched his teeth as he eased his cock into the very tight muscles. "Relax and let me in. It will feel so fucking good, baby. You'll be filled in every hole by your men."

He eased deeper and deeper until he felt the "plop" sensation, and then was fully seated in her ass. The three of them exhaled as Catalina moaned against Cody's cock.

In and out, they moved in sync, rocking the bed, thrusting into Catalina's body.

"Here I come, baby. Here I come," Cody said and then thrust and came in her mouth. She licked him clean, and he moved off the bed.

"Too fucking tight. Holy hell, baby, this ass of yours is fucking gripping my cock so tight. I'm coming," Jeremy said and began to move faster and faster.

"Oh God!"

She screamed her release, and Jeremy came pumping into her ass three more times. Then, holding himself inside of her as he pressed his body against hers and cupped her breasts, he tweaked the nipples then kissed her everywhere his mouth could reach.

He eased out of her ass, and Cooper continued to thrust up into her. Then Don stood up.

"What do you think you're doing?" Jeremy asked as Don rolled a condom onto his cock.

"I'm making love to our woman tonight, too."

He eased around her and grabbed the tube of lube, then pressed some into her ass. A moment later, he was massaging her back and whispering to her.

"I need inside of you, baby. Tonight you become all of ours."

"Be careful, Don. Please, the stitches," she said with concern, but then she gasped as Don eased his cock into her ass and thrust all the way in.

"Holy fuck," Don said, gripping her hips and tilting his head back.

Cooper moaned and thrust along with him.

"I'm coming, bud. I'm fucking coming," Cooper exclaimed and then thrust upward, wrapping his arms around Catalina to pull her close before he covered her mouth and kissed her deeply.

Don thrust faster and faster.

"Don, oh God, you're so hard. This is so wild. I'm coming again. Oh!" She cried out, and so did Don as they came simultaneously.

* * * *

Catalina collapsed against Cooper's chest as Don eased out of her. Jeremy was there to help his brother lie back down on the bed. There were a lot of grunts and mumbled "fucks" as everyone calmed their breathing. Catalina felt sedated. She'd done it. She'd allowed four men to make love to her together, and looking at each of them, she figured she was a very lucky woman indeed.

Cooper rolled her to the side, sliding his cock out from her pussy. She moaned softly, and then Cody was there with a warm washcloth and began to wash her up. She grabbed for the cloth.

"I can do that."

Cooper tightened his hold and rolled her to her back, placing one of his legs over her left thigh as Cody cleaned her up, then kissed her pussy.

"It's our job to take care of our woman," Cooper said firmly.

Her cheeks blushed, and her belly did a series of flips and flops from his possessive words.

"That was amazing, Catalina. Thank you for trusting us and letting us in."

"I can't believe we just did that," Catalina said. She couldn't resist running her fingers through Cooper's hair and feeling the slight bit of stubble on his cheeks.

He lowered his mouth to hers and kissed her. "You're so damn special, baby. Damn special."

"And so are the four of you," she said, and then closed her eyes and absorbed every moment of contentedness she felt right now.

* * * *

"Do you have to go?" Cooper whispered to Catalina as she tiptoed out of Don's room after checking on him and the bandage. He'd watched her kiss Don's forehead and then smile at him before she met Cooper at the doorway.

"He needs to rest, and I have plans this morning," she told him, and he took her hand, brought it to his lips, and kissed her fingertips.

Cooper pressed her against the wall, maneuvered his thigh between her legs, and absorbed the feel of her in his arms. He didn't want her to leave. He wanted everything instantly, a house, her living with them, a family, all of it. Cooper started to kiss along her neck and suckle her skin. He felt her grip his arms as he ran his hand under her dress to her hip.

"Stay, baby. Don't leave."

"Cooper, I stayed last night. I have these plans with my friends."

"Ditch them and stay with us," Cody added, and Cooper chuckled against her neck. He felt her shiver.

When Cooper pulled back, she cupped his cheeks then ran her hands through his hair. "I would love to stay, but I just can't. Besides, Jeremy and Cody came to see you guys and spend some time together. I'll call you tonight."

"Where are you going?" Cody asked with his arms crossed in front of his chest.

Cooper pulled back, and she straightened out her dress.

"To register for the 10K race next Saturday morning, then to lunch with friends, and I think the Station later tonight, but I'm not sure yet. Shayla, MaryAnn, and Destiny want to go to this new club in Fairway."

"New club? Which one?" Cooper asked her.

"The Water Crest Yacht Club. Destiny's cousin works at the place, and she said the tiki bar and live band are supposed to be phenomenal."

"So you're going there with them and Serefina, too?" Cooper asked her.

"No, just Shayla, MaryAnn, and Destiny. Serefina and the girls are meeting for lunch." She ran her palms up his chest and then looked at Cody.

"Why are you looking at me like that?" she asked, and Cooper released her, but he was feeling like Cody probably was, unsure and a bit jealous, as he looked at her long blonde hair and gorgeous blue eyes.

"Come here," Cody said with his arms still crossed until Catalina slowly walked toward him. Cody caressed her cheek. When she reached up and held his wrist and arm, then closed her eyes as if relishing the feel of Cody's touch, Cooper felt even more protective.

"I thought we would take this time to spend together?" Cody whispered. She stepped closer and placed her hand on his chest as she looked way up at him. She was so petite compared to each of them. They towered over her.

"I made these plans a week ago. Besides, you and Jeremy came here to see Don and Cooper. It's a good time to catch up and talk things over. I'll see you soon."

"Tomorrow? You'll spend the entire day and night with us tomorrow?" he asked.

Cooper waited for her response, and just then, Jeremy walked into the hallway after showering.

"I think we can do that."

Cody pulled her close. He had one arm wrapped around her waist with his palm half over her ass, and the other cupped her hair and cheek. "Definitely we're doing that. What time should we pick you up tomorrow?"

"All depends on how late I get in tonight," she replied.

"Late? Where are you going?" Jeremy asked.

"She has plans with friends to go to some fancy yacht club," Cooper told his brother.

"We're not going to see you tonight? What about Don? He might need you," Jeremy added, and Cooper was surprised. It seemed to him that Cody and Jeremy really liked Catalina. In fact, they were acting even more possessive and protective than he was.

"Jeremy, he'll be fine. He has all the information and care instructions the doctor gave him, plus his experience and Cooper's with first aid. I'll miss all of you if that makes you feel better."

Cooper nuzzled against her neck and began kissing her skin. "Stay longer." He ran his hands up her dress and over her ass. He pressed her hard against him before he moved his mouth from her neck to her jaw and then her mouth.

When he lifted her up and pressed her against the wall with her straddling his hips, Cooper got all excited and felt needy all over again.

"Cody." She gasped, pulling her mouth from his, as Cody appeared to be fingering her cunt. The material of the dress covered her, but one look at her head tilted back, her blotchy chest, and Cody's arm moving back and forth and Cooper knew he was fingering their woman.

"Cody. Oh God, Cody, please."

"Come for me, sugar. Come all over my fingers. Let me take you right here against the wall. I need you."

* * * *

Catalina gasped as Cody fingered her pussy and pressed her against the wall. She felt so aroused and needy. The truth was she didn't want to go out today or tonight. She wanted to be here with her men, but she also felt as though they needed time to talk and she needed a little space to comprehend what had taken place between them last night and this morning.

She felt Cody remove his fingers and then unzip his pants.

"Cody," she whispered as he set her down, pushed down her panties, and picked her back up again.

"Condom, bro," Jeremy said, joining them with Cooper by the wall.

"Catalina?" Cody held her gaze.

"You don't need them. I'm on birth control," she told Cody.

"What?" Cooper and Jeremy asked at the same time.

Cody's expression changed. He looked so carnal and wild.

"Fuck yeah. No barriers. I get to feel you completely." He stroked up into her cunt. She gripped his shoulders, tilted her head back, and moaned at the instant fullness she felt.

Cody thrust into her, and she counter-thrust against him as she ran her fingers through his hair and held on for the ride. He was relentless with his strokes, and the feel of his large, hard hands squeezing her ass and her thighs, widening them so he could get deeper, made her lose her breath.

"Cody!" She screamed out his name as she came so hard she shook in his arms.

Cody continued to thrust and grunt her name. "Catalina, Catalina. Oh God, baby. Fuck." He roared and came inside of her, filling her with his seed.

In her mind, she imagined being pregnant, bearing their children and being a family. The thoughts struck a sore spot in her heart. Her own flesh and blood, her sister, had betrayed her, hurt her over a man. Could Cody, Jeremy, Don, and Cooper be trusted to belong to only her, or could another woman come along and take them away from her just like her sister had taken away Paul?

She hugged Cody tight as the tears reached her eyes.

"Catalina?" he whispered and pulled back. He cupped her face. "Did I hurt you, baby?"

She shook her head. "No. No, Cody, that was beautiful," she whispered.

He slowly set her down and kissed her again.

Jeremy moved closer and took her hand. He looked at Cooper then back at her. "Coop and I need you, too, before you go."

"Jeremy, it's getting late," she said, but he cut her off and kissed her deeply. A moment later, he was picking her up and carrying her to another bedroom.

In a flash, they had her naked.

Jeremy lay on the bed, stroking his cock and curling his finger toward her. She smiled at him and that sexy, hard body, the determined look on his face, and a superiority that oozed from him. He was just so fine that she would follow his orders, his control any day of the week.

She crawled up on top of him, and he gripped her hips.

"We're going to give you something to remember us by tonight when you're out with your friends," Jeremy told her as he cupped her head and brought her down for a deep, sensual kiss. He ran his hand along her hip and over her ass, squeezing it hard and possessively.

Then she felt the hands on her ass, Cooper move in behind her, and then the cool liquid against her anus.

She pulled from Jeremy's mouth and gasped when Cooper pressed a finger into her ass.

"When guys come flirting with you, remember who you belong to, baby," Cooper said as he eased a finger in and out of her ass while he pressed over her and suckled her neck.

Jeremy lifted her hips and aligned his cock with her pussy. She felt so aroused, turned-on by their words and touch, that she lowered over Jeremy's large, thick cock and sank down, taking him deep.

"Fuck yeah, you feel so good. God, I love being inside of you without a condom. Holy fuck." Jeremy gripped her hips and pumped up into her slowly.

Behind her, Cooper removed his finger and placed the tip of his cock against her anus. He slowly began to breach her ass.

"No barriers. No walls or uncertainty that this is real, that we're meant to be. All of us together." He sank into her slowly as she gasped for air and moaned aloud. When she felt the "plop," all three of them moaned a sigh of contentedness, and she shivered as her pussy quaked.

In and out, they began to move in sync, one cock in her pussy and one in her ass. She held on to Jeremy's shoulders, locked gazes with his brown eyes, the control, the manliness, and authority in him so apparent even now in bed. He was a leader, a sexy, bossy federal agent, and she would be lying if she said it didn't make her wild. She pressed her ass back, and Cooper thrust into her harder.

Smack.

"Cooper!" she squealed.

Smack, smack, smack.

"This is our ass, our body. You belong to the four of us. Remember that, baby. You hear me?" he asked, his tone so hard, loud, and so wild that she felt her pussy explode.

"Yes. Yes, Cooper." She rocked back and forth, and Jeremy cupped her breasts. Cody joined them.

"Setting down the rules, brothers, so our woman knows she's all ours always?" he asked.

"Hell yeah," Cooper stated.

Catalina moaned and wiggled as both men continued to thrust into her body, and then Cody leaned over and suckled her breast that Jeremy held in offering. It was so sexy, naughty, the way they did that. Everything about them excited her. Their large hands, their take-charge attitudes, and the way they fed off one another's desires and need to possess her.

Cody tugged on her nipple, and she moaned.

"I'm there, baby. I'm so fucking there," Cooper said.

Smack.

He spanked her again, and she was shocked at how turned-on she was. She moaned and fell forward, and both men increased their pace.

"God, you're so beautiful. I love watching my brothers fuck you," Cody told her, and he cupped her cheeks and then plunged his tongue into her mouth.

Jeremy pinched her nipples and thrust upward hard while Cooper smacked her ass and thrust three more times before calling out her name.

Her body exploded again, and then Jeremy gripped her hips tightly and thrust upward hard.

"Ours. All fucking ours," Jeremy said.

Cody moved back, and she fell against Jeremy's chest. Cooper caressed her ass and kissed her shoulders and down her spine as he eased out of her ass.

Jeremy ran his hands along her back and then to her ass, squeezing it. She gasped. It felt tender, and Jeremy chuckled.

Cody reached over, and she felt his hands and then his mouth.

"A nice, pink ass. I love it. So fucking sexy, the way you came when he spanked you. You're made for us, that's for sure," Cody said, and she moaned.

"I don't even feel like moving," she whispered.

Jeremy caressed her hair from her cheek and kissed her temple. "Good. You can stay right here, and we can make love all day and all night."

She thought about that and would have loved to, but then her friends would be mad, and she would also be giving these guys way too much control over her too soon.

She rose up, and he raised one of his eyebrows at her.

She smiled. "It's better if I go. This is all so new, and I don't want to make the wrong choice. I promised my friends I would hang out with them today and tonight. I need to go." She kissed his lips and slowly sat up, but as she began to climb off of him, Jeremy gripped her hips and held her in place.

"This is special. It's real. We'll work things out, Catalina."

She gave him a smile and caressed his chest.

"Take the time to talk things over, and I'll call you tomorrow."

She got up, and Cooper was there, pulling her into his arms.

"You'll text us and let us know where you are and that you're okay, then again when you get home."

She ran her fingers through his hair and pressed her breasts against his chest.

"And if I'm really late getting home?"

Smack.

She gasped and pulled back and covered her ass with her hand. "Cody," she reprimanded.

"Watch it, you, or you'll get a spanking again tomorrow for naughty behavior."

Jeremy and Cooper laughed.

"Very funny, Cody." She grabbed her dress and headed toward the bathroom, but Cody came up behind her, lifted her up over his shoulder, and ran his hand along her ass.

"You're not leaving yet. I've got shower plans for us."

As he closed the door with his foot and turned on the shower, all while holding her over his shoulder as if she were light as a feather, she knew she was going to be late. In fact, it was going to take some serious discipline to get her to stick to her guns and not give in to their immediate demands and control, even though she loved every second of it.

Cody set her down and then brought her into the shower. He kissed her deeply and then began to slowly soap up her body. She leaned back with his instructions, closed her eyes, and exhaled, thinking maybe she could stay a little longer. Maybe their control and desire to be with her was exactly what she needed after all.

Chapter 3

The bar was noisy, but that background static somehow made it easier for them to discuss what was going on in their lives and get on board together.

"There are things we can look into doing. It's just going to take some time to work things out with the job," Cody said, and then he took a sip of beer while he and his brothers sat around a pub table at the Station. They had been talking about Catalina since she left this morning. Well, closer to noon. They would have preferred being with her tonight, but she did have a point about how fast things were moving.

"It's a lot to think about," Jeremy said, "but in a way, meeting Catalina and having such strong feelings equally makes the decision to make the changes in our life a little easier. I mean, I know I'll miss what I did, but it was dangerous. I dealt with a lot of heavy shit, and the fact that a few of those bad guys are still at large, even if they are out of the country, doesn't sit right with me, but I have to face the facts that the agency isn't going to spend money and time searching for those men when there are other, stronger threats. I guess it's time to move on, retire, and maybe settle down." Jeremy looked at each of his brothers before taking a slug of beer.

"I feel the same way," Cody said. "Yet, I don't want to give up this fight against terrorists and their threats. As I mentioned earlier, one of the main headquarters affiliated with my current office is a commute away from Treasure Town by thirty-five, forty minutes. I could look into openings there."

"This is great. It can work out, but we want the two of you to be one-hundred-percent certain. Even if it's a strain on this relationship, we can give the long-distance thing a shot. Cooper and I will be here, and you can drive out on weekends until you decide," Don told them.

"That's not fair. Not to you guys, to us, and especially not to Catalina. She's our woman now, and she must come first in everything we do. That's how our dads did it with Mom," Cooper told them.

"He's right, but we pretty much are agreeing and facing the fact that Catalina is the one for us, that she's special and we're willing to change our lives for her," Jeremy stated.

"For us. We deserve this. You guys deserve to be happy and for all of us to be together like we talked about. It's right," Cooper said to them.

"Now if only I can get rid of this sick feeling in the pit of my stomach, not having her here," Don said to them.

Cody exhaled and took a slug from his bottle of Bud.

"Fucking tell me about it. I can't stop thinking about where she is and who she's with, and if she's safe or if some guys are hitting on her. She's so beautiful and sexy. God, I've never felt jealous before. It sucks."

Jeremy looked at his cell phone. "Nothing yet."

"It's kind of funny how she looks to you as the leader of this family," Don said to Jeremy.

"Well, he's always been on top of things and leading the way. Calmed each of us down when we could have lost our cool and gotten in serious trouble," Cooper said.

"How do you explain Cody, then, and his little juvenile record?" Don asked.

Jeremy and Cooper chuckled.

"He's an overachiever and has always had a problem with authority. All those crazy obsessions with guns, blowing shit up, and running secret missions through the neighborhood came in handy in the military and even now are incorporated into his position fighting terrorists," Jeremy said, and they chuckled.

"Don't rank on me because Catalina is completely turned on by my macho aggressiveness, especially in the bedroom. If it weren't for me, the two of you wouldn't have gotten to make love to her again this morning," Cody teased.

"He has a point, and somehow he got to make love to her twice, too."

"Do we really need to talk about this? I was fucking out cold from the painkillers she made me take," Don said, sounding upset.

"Well, she did have to coax you into it," Jeremy reminded him, and Cody laughed.

Don hadn't wanted to take the painkillers, but his leg was throbbing, and she told him it would help with the achiness. She fed him the pill and gave him a sip of water, then unzipped his pants and sucked his cock until he came. It had been fucking incredible to watch. The thought had Cody missing Catalina entirely too much.

"Need you remind us of that?" Cooper asked and shook his head.

Cody laughed.

"We are so screwed. Why hasn't she texted yet?"

* * * *

Catalina was smiling and laughing with Shayla, MaryAnn, and Destiny. They were dancing to the music as they stood by the tiki bar talking about the place and about the large boats that docked nearby.

She missed the guys, but after talking to Michaela today about how fast things were moving, she'd shared her own experience and said that taking time to breathe and do things with other people like her friends was important and the men would learn to understand. Catalina thought about that, and maybe the guys were being extra protective and wanting all their time with her because Jeremy and

Cody were only here for a short time. Actually, she didn't know how long they would be here and had never asked.

She felt a little sick to her stomach and then realized that she hadn't texted them. She took out her phone and pulled up Jeremy's number. It was so odd how she saw him as the leader of the four brothers. He just had such a strong character and seemed mysterious in some ways, and his brothers tended to follow his lead. She smiled.

"I need to text the guys really quick," she told the girls.

"Oh boy, are they the jealous type?" Shayla teased. "Damn, I bet they are. The twins look super intense, and I heard how hard they are on the firefighters during training."

"I heard the rookie that hit Don with the Halligan got his ass reamed out by Cooper," Destiny told them.

"Well, I think Catalina hit the jackpot with all four of them. Cody and Jeremy look so dangerous and mysterious. I bet they're considered human lethal weapons," MaryAnn added, and they continued to carry on about Catalina's men.

Catalina shook her head and walked away from them toward the side by the docks where the boats came in. People were pulling up, and others were leaving. The Water Crest Yacht Club was very crowded and popular with boaters and even some wealthy snobs who thought they could do as they pleased. Destiny's cousin introduced them to a group of guys and some women, and in a matter of ten minutes, Catalina and her friends made excuses to head to the tiki bar.

She texted a message to the guys and then waited for their response. As she looked out across the water, she thought it was a beautiful night as the sun set, appearing as if it fell into the water on the horizon. She felt so different. Even looking around the town earlier today had seemed different. She realized instantly that it was because of Cooper, Don, Cody, and Jeremy. They set her heart on fire. They made her feel things no other man ever had. In fact, she was pretty sure she was falling in love with them.

That made her feel panicked a moment and worry about making a mistake. Was it right? Would it last? What if loving four men didn't work out? She would be left as used goods, a woman who'd had sex with four men at once. God, she prayed she didn't make a mistake. That little ache of insecurity from the past began to vibrate from deep within.

"Cat?"

She heard her name and instantly felt the tightness hit her chest. Her mouth opened, and her mind juggled for the words to reply as Paul, her ex from college, appeared there in front of her. He smiled wide as he and a few friends stopped. They all looked her over. She swallowed hard. What were the chances of seeing him here tonight? What should she do? *Oh God, he looks good. Different, older, mature.* She could do this. She had prepared for this moment for years. She wasn't the hurt, used, naive woman any longer.

"Paul, my God, what are you doing here?"

He stared at her, looked over her body, and she was so glad she'd worn the tight-fitting dress that hugged her curves and brought out the blue in her eyes. The top dipped a little low, and she felt self-conscious about it, thinking that Cody would have flipped out for her wearing it without him. That thought made her smile inside. She was so hooked on them.

Paul looked at his friends, and they gave his arm a tap. "Who is this?" one asked.

"Oh, how rude of me. This is Catalina. We went to college together," he said, and she saw the looks his friends gave her.

"Catalina? Really? Wow." One licked his lips as he stared at her chest. She felt a bit embarrassed, and as if she possible could have been the topic of his and his friends' female-partner sex stories. It hurt to think that maybe Paul had said things about her, and the fact she'd given him her virginity and they'd been boyfriend and girlfriend for four years. Well, lovers who planned on spending the rest of their lives together.

"Give me a few minutes. I'll meet you guys up there," he said to them.

"Nice to meet you, Catalina. You should join us and hang out," one of them said.

"I'm here with friends, but thanks," she replied with not as much confidence as she hoped her voice would send.

Someone walked behind Paul and bumped him along with a crowd of other boaters. She stepped back, and he stepped closer to her, touching her hip and holding her gaze. She stared at him. Those big blue eyes, the shaggy blond hair, the whole wealthy, sophisticated doctor. What was he doing here?

"God, Catalina, you look incredible. How are you? What have you been up to? My God, I've thought about you so much over the years and wondered where you'd disappeared to."

He licked his lower lip, and she suddenly felt that sensation, the one where she was talking to a guy and she could tell that sex was the only thing on his mind.

"I'm doing great. What are you doing around here?" she asked.

"I'm on a long weekend from the city. I work in Manhattan now. I have my own practice with two of my colleagues, the two you met and asked if you could join us. Are you sure you can't? I'd love to catch up. Talk old times."

He reached out and caressed her hair from her cheek. She was a bit nervous. He touched her like he had every right to, like what happened between them years ago gave him a right to do as he pleased. She began to remember things about their relationship and, of course, what had ultimately destroyed their future..

She chuckled low and pulled back. "Seriously?" she asked, feeling a mix of emotions. There were those old feelings, the attraction she had, and the fact that she'd given so much to this man and spent four years of her life loving him and worshipping the ground he walked on. Then there was the hurt, the pain of him cheating on her with her sister. It had killed her inside. She had just graduated and been offered a job in the hospital near school, but he was interning there, so she had declined and left completely. She'd disappeared and headed back toward her grandparents' home in Treasure Town.

He squinted at her.

"What? Did I say something wrong?"

"Listen, it's nice to see you and hear that you're doing well. That's the kind response I have to you because I'm older, more mature, and have a better understanding of men like you. I don't want to catch up, talk old times, and act like what you did never happened. I'm here with friends. I have to go."

She decided it was better to walk away, pretend to be tough instead of allowing those old insecure feelings to work her over. He always had a hold on her heart. She'd come so close to forgiving him and what he'd done, but just as she was about to try again with him, the situation with her sister had gotten worse.

He grabbed her arm to stop her, and she paused and looked up at him. His blue eyes bore into hers. There was that look, that deep, controlling, hard expression that used to turn her on and make her feel like his treasure, his possession, and every desire.

"You can't be angry at me for what happened. It was six years ago. It was the biggest mistake of my life, Catalina. I lost you because of one stupid fucking night and too much alcohol."

She looked around them.

"Let go of my arm. I don't have anything to say to you. It happened. We all moved on, and you appear to be just fine, Paul."

He released her arm and exhaled, then ran his fingers through his hair.

"If you had taken my calls, if you'd let me explain what happened, then maybe things could have worked out differently."

"I doubt that, Paul. There was no room for forgiveness then." She looked around her. "Where is the little wife, anyway?"

She saw his face change instantly at the mention of Kaylee. She could actually see his eyes fill up, and she wondered if something bad had happened to her. She wouldn't even know because they'd stopped talking years ago when Kaylee had slept with Paul and gotten pregnant. She had been contemplating forgiving him and trying to work things out because she knew her sister was spoiled and a manipulator. She thought the world owed her everything because she was alive, and because their parents had died and their grandmother had been left to raise them.

But then her sister called her crying and saying she was pregnant and that Paul was the father. The knife they stuck in her heart felt as if it had twisted and gone even deeper. She would never forget the pain or the shock. She gulped down the lump of emotion and then came the care, the empathy for someone in need. It was her instinct, her character.

"What happened?" she asked.

He looked around them, took her arm, and they stepped to the side by a high bar table near the dock.

"I know what I did was unforgiveable. I slept with your sister. I was your boyfriend. We made plans to get married and to get work at the same hospital. I fucked up that night, and I know I hurt you and so did your sister."

"I don't talk to her. I haven't since that morning I walked in—"

She turned away, the hurt obviously still burning deep in her soul as she remembered that morning. They'd graduated that week, and there had been lots of parties. Her sister visited. She always liked to come up to the college and hang out, and she'd even met a guy there.

"I don't know how to explain this other than to tell you that the baby wasn't mine."

"What?" she asked.

"Your sister and I slept together that night, but apparently, she was already pregnant. By Dave Walters."

"The mechanic from Westfield where we grew up?"

He exhaled and ran his fingers through his blond, shaggy hair. Now with a closer look, she could see how he had aged some. Maybe being a medical doctor, a surgeon, or because of what her sister had put him through. He began to explain how he found out, how the baby had a medical condition that usually comes from the father and that he didn't have it. No male in his family had it.

"There were little things she said, and then I was working a lot of hours and sometimes I would come home and find out that your grandmother had had the baby all weekend. Anyway, within a year, she came clean because we had blood work done, and, well, I had them do a paternity test. It was very clear I wasn't the father. I confronted her on it, and she said she didn't want to end up married to some blue-collar guy and struggle to make ends meet when her sister was going to marry a doctor and be rich and have everything."

"That's Kaylee. Forget about love, about caring for someone because it's the right thing to do. She would always ask—"

"What's in it for me?" he said the words, and she realized that he had suffered greatly. He had been fooled by Kaylee, roped into thinking he'd gotten her pregnant and that he'd done the right thing and married her and tried to raise a baby, only to find out she'd lied and it wasn't his. How sad.

"You moved on with your life. You're still in the medical field?" she asked.

"I work as a cardiologist at Hospital for Special Surgery. I love it. I'm busy all the time, and I have a great staff of nurses, although I always imagined I'd have you by my side helping." He winked.

She smiled as she thought about those days and what they'd shared.

"Things change and happen for a reason, Paul."

He reached up and cupped her cheek.

"Like seeing you here tonight after all these years. What we had was so special. If I could turn back the hands of time, Catalina, I would change that moment, that night I drank too much and fucked up. My God, you look so beautiful."

She lowered her head. She couldn't believe this was happening to her. If they had met any time sooner, would she have forgiven him and tried to work things out this many years later? She knew the answer would be yes because she was feeling lonely and as if leaving Treasure Town was her only option. Then she'd met Jeremy and his brothers at the hospital, and she held on to the hope she would see them again, but they didn't come back to ask her out. Time passed, and she thought maybe there was no man out there who could truly love her, be trustworthy, and put her first.

But she hadn't met Paul like this earlier, weeks ago. Here he was now and at a time she was trying to figure out what she wanted to do with her life, if she could risk her heart on four men who were unstable in their careers, who wanted to share her, and who also would be split apart because Cody and Jeremy still lived in New York. How would it all work out?

This situation, this reminder of the pain, of not being able to keep Paul interested in only her, just made her wonder how she would keep four strikingly handsome men like Cooper, Cody, Don, and Jeremy happy. They weren't even sure what they wanted to do with their lives and were in a transitional stage. They might have to give a long-distance relationship a try for a while. What if it didn't work out? But she cared for them so much. She could see herself loving them if she could just let go of the fear from her past.

"Catalina?" he whispered. "It's good we met tonight out of the blue." He smiled.

"I think so, too."

"Can I buy you a drink and we can talk some more?"

She heard her phone buzzing again and knew she had another text message.

"I don't think so. I think seeing you, hearing what happened, puts a lot of things in perspective for me. I had a hard time all these years moving on, Paul, and trusting another man, but just recently I found myself in the kind of relationship where trust is earned and the connection is so strong that I feel I can take a chance. It was nice seeing you, though. I wish you all the best. I need to get back to my friends."

She stared to turn away, and he grabbed her arm tightly, pulling her closer, catching her off–guard, making her collide against his chest. It was so fast, so unexpected as he reached under her hair and neck, pulled her roughly to him, and kissed her. He plunged his tongue in deep and ran his hands along her ass, squeezing her to him, and she struggled to get free. She pinched his side, making him release her lips, and then pushed him away.

He grabbed her arm and tried pulling her down the dock toward the boats. She planted her heels, but the sandals slid along the wood.

"Catalina, stay. Come back to my boat with me. We'll talk some more. Have a good time." He pulled her close and started to rub along her back. She was pressed up against his chest.

"Let go of me, Paul. Nothing is ever going to happen between us. Let it go."

He shook his head and suddenly looked so different, so angry, and bad thoughts went through her mind. He wasn't the same young man in college she had fallen in love with.

"Don't do this, Paul. We can end this on a friendly, civilized level, or it can end badly."

He pressed his mouth to her neck and ear. He held her so tightly she couldn't move or breathe. She pressed her hands against him, trying to push him away. Then she felt his heavy breathing against her ear and neck.

"You were a way better fuck than your sister. I bet you're even better now."

"Catalina, what's going on?" Shayla asked as she, Destiny, and MaryAnn approached. Catalina was so relieved to see her friends and so angry at his words. He pulled slightly back at the unexpected interruption, and Catalina made her move.

"Let go of me, you piece of crap." She pushed away, and he gripped her wrist tightly.

"Come with me now," he demanded, pulling her along the dock, and she heard her friends yelling for him to let go of her.

Catalina made a fist as anger filled her belly, and she decked him right in the nose. Blood splattered, hitting her dress, causing a scene as her friends gasped, and then Paul carried on, calling her names and saying she was a whore like her sister.

"Let's go," Catalina said and then held her hand to her chest as Paul's friends came to his aid. He pushed them off and carried on about needing ice. She went right to the bar with her friends.

"I think that calls for some shots," she said, and the girls bombarded her with questions as the bartender got her ice and Destiny's friends who worked there kicked Paul and his crew of friends out.

She was so angry she saw red as she tried to calm her breathing. She'd fallen for his charms, his sad story, and then he tried to talk her into going to his boat. Like she would just forget all the pain and betrayal she'd felt and let him fuck her on a boat? Asshole.

She was carrying on in her head and then filling her friends in on the entire story.

"Here, take the shot," Destiny said. "There's more lined up. That shit calls for a celebration. You've moved on and have four men that adore you. Forget about Paul, your sister, and all that drama. You're living in Treasure Town. Life is going to be perfect from here on out."

She and Destiny clinked the shots together and drank them down fast. Then she looked at her hand and felt it throbbing. It was already bruising and ached, but she felt good, empowered, and as if there was a clean slate. What happened in the past was in the past. Cody, Cooper, Jeremy, and Don were her future, and nothing would stand in the way.

* * * *

Clover watched the blonde. She was a very attractive woman and apparently was romantically involved with Agent Jones and his brothers. She handled herself well against the blond man. It was obvious that they knew one another, but things had turned ugly fast. Her quick reflexes and right hook warned Clover to not underestimate her if his boss chose to go after her to get to Jeremy Jones. He was going to make the call soon. The choice of who got hurt, who lived, and who died would be in Jeremy's hands. Frederick Price was smart, and he wanted revenge and would get it. Clover just needed to wait to see what exactly his boss had in mind.

He walked out of the yacht club and headed to his car when his cell phone rang.

"Hello."

"I've got another agent you can use to get those names we need, but you need to move quickly," Frederick told him.

"What about Agent Jones?"

"Him I want to suffer. I want to hit him where it hurts and watch him beg for mercy. He'll pay the ultimate price for destroying our operation. Everyone else has moved on, but not me. It ends with me and Agent Jones. I'll send you the address and information."

He disconnected the call and Clover waited for the text. When he got it, he smiled. Looked like he was heading to New York to kill some agents.

* * * *

Catalina went jogging in the morning, even though she felt terrible. She wasn't hung-over, but she had drunk a lot and her hand was all bruised from decking Paul. She worried about telling the guys what had happened, but as she'd bumped into Bull on her way back from the boardwalk, it appeared that word spread quickly about the incident.

Apparently when Destiny's cousins and the owners of the yacht club wanted them thrown out, Paul's snobby friends called the police and complained, then tried to act as if they would press charges, but they got Jake on the phone, and he had already heard from Michaela about what happened from Serefina, who heard from Eddie and Lance Martelli, who knew the bartender's brother Al who worked at Sullivan's. Treasure Town was indeed a small town, and so was Fairway right next door.

As she rounded the corner to where her townhouse was, she saw the familiar big blue truck and cringed. She had been sure to text the guys and let them know she'd gotten in late last night. When they asked if everything was okay, she lied and said it was good and then went for a jog. Obviously word had traveled, and now she would have to explain what happened.

She was surprised that they were nowhere in sight, and as she unlocked the door to her townhouse, there they were, standing or sitting around her kitchen and living room, and boy, did they look pissed.

She closed the door and placed her hands on her hips. She cringed as she forgot about her bruised hand.

"How did you get in here?" she asked.

They looked at her as if it was the stupidest question, and she realized it was.

She forgot what kind of men she was talking to as she pulled her lips tight and then walked toward the kitchen.

Jeremy spoke up first. "We were worried about you. We tried calling you several times."

"I was out jogging. It's my last chance to practice before next Saturday and the race." She took a slug of water from the water bottle.

"Enough of the bullshit. What the fuck happened last night? Were you even going to tell us about this asshole who bothered you? About how he was going to press charges? What the hell went down and why didn't you call us?" Cody asked, raising his voice.

She looked at him as she set the bottle down on the counter.

"I took care of it," she said to him.

They were obviously shocked at her response. None of them replied for a moment.

"I really need to shower and change," she said.

"Let's see the hand," Cooper said to her.

"It's no big deal. It's not even sore," she said, and he touched it, taking it into his hand. She gasped and pulled back.

"Jesus, it's fucking sore and badly bruised. Are you certain you didn't break it?" he asked, and this time she gave him a smartass expression.

"Who the hell was this guy? What happened?" Don asked, and she took a deep breath before she explained.

"Why didn't you tell us about this guy and your sister? Is this why you were adamant about not getting involved with all of us at this point?" Cooper asked her.

"Yes. It hurt so badly when I found them in bed together. We had our whole lives planned out, and my own sister sleeps with my boyfriend. I trusted him, and I trusted her."

"I'm certain it did hurt. I couldn't even imagine that. We would never hurt you, Catalina. We all want you as our woman," Cooper told her.

She stepped back and walked over to the couch. She sat on the arm of it and looked at the four of them.

"It's been so hard for me over the years since that happened. I was in love with Paul. We planned our whole lives together, and that night, in some drunken stupor, he slept with Kaylee. It hurt badly, and for weeks he would call and try to talk with me and beg for forgiveness." She looked down at her hands and felt the tears in her eyes. "I almost forgave him. God knows what that weakness would have cost me in the long run. But then Kaylee told him she was pregnant."

"Damn, that's why you don't talk to your sister or other family?"

"There is no other family, Cody. My grandmother passed away last year."

"So this guy sees you after all this time and you start talking to him? Did you still have feelings for him?" Jeremy asked her.

She shook her head. "I broke his damn nose, Jeremy. What do you think?" she replied sarcastically.

"You already have one spanking coming your way for not calling us immediately last night. You want to make it multiple?" Cooper asked her as he crossed his arms in front of his chest. His tone, his appearance, and words should have made her angry or even worried, but they didn't. She felt aroused and in such need of them, but she was fighting it. She was fearful she could get hurt again and, this time, it would be quadruple the pain.

She swallowed hard.

"I admit I felt badly as he explained what happened and how the baby turned out not to be his." She went on to tell them exactly what had taken place and led up to her slugging him.

Cody ran his fingers through his hair. "And he was trying to press charges against you? He could have forced you onto a boat with those guys and raped you." He raised his voice.

"I know, Cody."

"No, I don't think you realize how fucked up this is and how serious of a situation you were involved in. Why would you talk to him? I know you're a sweet person with a big heart, but seriously, Catalina, why?" he asked as he approached her. He knelt down in front of her, took her hand, brought it to his lips, and kissed the bruising.

"I was confused, and I wasn't really paying attention to the signs because I kept thinking about how it all happened, and about my fears. I hadn't been with any other man since Paul until the four of you. That's four older, more experienced men, and I'm scared, Cody. I'm scared of falling so fast, of trusting each of you entirely in case you can't work things out and move here to Treasure Town, and I'm scared because I already love each of you, and I shouldn't."

The tears filled her eyes, and Cody pulled her into his arms and hugged her tightly.

"I know you're scared. We are, too. We're taking huge risks as well and moving our world to be with you here. Cooper and I are taking the job offer. Cody and Jeremy are looking into other options for work nearby here. Today we're looking at houses, and we want you to come with us because it's going to be your house, too."

She pulled back, caught off-guard at his words.

"What?" she asked Cody, and he smirked, then looked at his brothers. She glanced at them as they stood there watching her.

"It's true. We're looking at houses, seeing how we can work this out," Jeremy told her.

Cody cupped her cheeks and looked into her eyes.

"You're not the only one who is scared or the only one who's fallen in love. We have, too." He pressed his lips to hers and kissed her deeply. When he released her lips, she wrapped her arms around his shoulders and hugged him tightly.

"I'm sorry I didn't call you. I'm sorry I freaked out and pushed you away. I want this to work. I need this to work because I need all four of you in my life."

"And we need you, but you're still getting an ass-spanking," Cooper said as he approached. Cody got up, and Cooper pulled her up into his arms. He kissed her deeply and then carried her toward her bedroom.

Her heart felt light. Love soared through her, and she wanted nothing more than to live happily ever after with her four sexy, hot men.

Catalina gasped when Cooper dropped her onto the bed.

He reached for her shorts and began pulling them down.

"Oh God, wait. I need to shower first. I'm all sweaty from my run."

"No need. A spanking first, and then we're going to get really sweaty anyway, baby. We've got three hours until we need to meet the real estate agent, Sophia," Cody said as he slapped a tube of lube in his hand and smiled wide.

Her anus clenched, and her pussy dripped cream.

She gasped as Cooper stripped her of her clothing and then tossed her onto her belly over his knees.

"Here's for not calling your men immediately last night."

Smack.

"Oh." She gasped and then felt his palm rub over the ache he'd caused.

"For making us worry all night, and then not calling us and telling us what happened last night, and how scared you were."

Smack.

She jerked and then felt the caress right before his fingers dipped into her very wet cunt.

"Oh God, Cooper."

Smack, smack, smack.

"You're our woman, and we're here to protect you and love you. Never forget that," Jeremy said as he undressed along with the others.

Smack.

"Oh God, please," she begged as Cody stroked her pussy and the men took turns smacking her ass.

In a flash, Cody lifted her up and placed her right on top of Don, who lay on the bed naked, his leg still bandaged.

She gripped his shoulders and lifted up. "Don, your stitches."

"I'm fucking fine. I need you. Ride me now. Prove to me that I'm yours and you're mine." He pulled her down for a kiss as she eased her pussy over his cock, taking him inside of her deeply. He released her lips, and they both sighed. "Heaven. Inside of you is fucking heaven, woman."

Then she felt the hands caressing her spine and then her ass.

"Fucking this ass is heaven," Cody whispered and then suckled a sensitive spot against her neck. She shivered and shook, making her pussy cream some more.

Then she felt Cody lift back, and a moment later, cool liquid pressed into her ass. She spread her thighs wider as she rocked her hips and fucked Don. Don cupped her breasts and pinched her nipples.

"So beautiful and giving. You're ours now. This body, your heart, and soul belong to us as ours belong to you," he said, and then she felt the fingers under her chin and Jeremy was there, stroking his cock.

She lowered her mouth immediately to his cock and began to suck him into her mouth. When Jeremy fisted her hair and began to stroke into her mouth, she relaxed her body and let them take her, control her, and love her. Then she felt fingers stroking her ass. Cody was there arousing her and getting her ass ready for cock. She wanted it, needed it, as she moaned against Jeremy's cock.

A moment later, Cody eased his fingers out and replaced them with his thick, hard muscle. The tip of his cock pressed through the tight rings, landing deeply inside of her ass with a plop as they all moaned together. In and out he stroked her ass while Don thrust upward, holding her hips tightly.

Her hand ached, but she didn't care. She was lost with her men inside her as she sucked Jeremy faster and faster, wanting to taste his essence and make him wild.

"Fuck, baby, slow down. Slow—"

He jerked his hips, and she held his cock deeply, relaxed her throat, and swallowed Jeremy's cum. He slowly pulled out and caressed her cheeks, then kissed her. "You'll pay for that later."

Smack.

She gasped as he spanked her ass and moved off the bed.

"Fuck, you had to do that," Cody said, and thrust again and again, then exploded in her ass.

He kissed her back as Don held her tightly while he stared up into her eyes and they made love slowly. But then she felt the cool liquid to her ass again and knew it was Cooper.

"Get ready, baby. You've got me all fired up, and looking at this nice, pink ass, knowing how turned-on a spanking made you, has me thinking wild thoughts."

Smack, smack, smack.

"Cooper!" she exclaimed.

"Fuck, Coop, I won't last if you keep that up," Don said with his teeth clenched.

Catalina eased her ass back as she rocked her hips and widened her thighs over Don. As Cooper pressed his cock to her anus, he spread her ass cheeks and gripped them hard.

"Fuck, whatever you do to make this ass this perfect, baby, keep doing it. I love it." He thrust fully into her ass, overwhelming her.

She gasped, and then she came hard, shaking on top of Don.

"Let's do her, Don. We've got three hours to make her see she belongs to us and that they'll never be any others but the Jones brothers."

She was lost in the sensations as Don began to thrust up into her while Cody and Jeremy cheered them on, taking front-row seats on the bed, watching and participating. Jeremy and Cody would pinch her nipple or grip her hair, then kiss her hard on the mouth while Cooper and Don fucked her good and hard. It was exhausting, and surprisingly she came again and again until Don and Cooper came inside of her together. She collapsed against Don's chest and let her men take care of her.

She couldn't move a muscle, but as strong lips kissed her bruised hand and other hands cleaned her up and kissed along her ass, she smiled wide.

"I could get used to this really fast," she said, and they chuckled.

"So could we," Jeremy said, and she blinked her eyes open to find them all there watching her and smiling.

Life was perfect, and absolutely nothing would make this go wrong. Nothing.

Chapter 4

Jeremy stood outside on the back deck of the house his brothers were renting.

"Say that again?" Jeremy asked the agents who headed the division he was part of.

"Will Mathews is dead. His body was found in a junkyard about twenty miles from his home. There are others, too." Special Agent Roman Spelling told him.

"Jesus. Any leads?"

"None, but the thing is, his computer and his passwords were used to log in sometime during his death. Classified documents were taken. As our IT guys look into deciphering what files exactly, we already know for sure that eight agents have been identified, their covers blown, and we're in the process of moving them immediately out of their undercover positions. It's bad, Jeremy. Your name was in that file, too, even though you've been pulled now for several months."

"Did you get all the agents out in time?" he asked, and Roman was quiet. "Roman, what the fuck? Just tell me. Did you get them all out of their undercover assignments before their covers were blown?"

"No. Four dead so far. We have had no further contact with the other four, but they could still be alive and on the run."

"Were they working the same case or similar ones? Is that the connection?"

"It's still part of the mess from Mateo's operation you took down with those friends of yours. This drug and weapons smuggling is huge and went further. We thought it died down, considering Castella and Fredrick Price disappeared, but our intel claims both men are still alive, Jeremy. This is looking like some form of revenge on our agency. You need to watch your ass. They have your file. They know where you live. Hell, they could already have made an attempt at trying to hurt you."

"I would know if they had. I need to protect my family. Any leads on where Frederick is operating from?"

"We've got men working on that now. Whoever killed Williams was a bit sloppy. The prints found on the body and at the scene are being run through the system. As soon as I hear anything, I'll call you. Are you at home?"

"No, I'm away someplace safe for now. My place should get looked at."

"I'll send some people. I'll be in touch. Watch your back, Jeremy. Until we can figure out who is responsible and identify them, they can come at you from any direction."

"I'll take precautions. Let me know how it goes at the house and any updates. I'll work on this end too."

Jeremy disconnected the call and ran his fingers through his hair. He hung his head as fear consumed him. He was putting his family, his woman, in jeopardy by being here. He had to leave.

"Jeremy?"

He heard Cody's voice and then turned to look at him.

His expression intensified. There was no holding back or lying to his brothers, and Cody knew the deal with this type of job.

"What the fuck happened? How bad?"

"Close the door," he told him, and Cody did, leaving Catalina and their brothers inside where they were making dinner together.

"I think it's best if I leave," he said after he explained to Cody what he'd just heard and what was going on.

"Do you really think that's a smart idea? At least I'm here to cover your back, as are the others in town. If you head back home, they could be waiting for you. This is fucking serious shit, Jeremy. They want to kill you."

Jeremy took a deep breath, released it, and thought about Catalina and his brothers. "I have to focus on Catalina and the three of you. I won't put any of you in danger, especially not her. I'll come back when it blows over and we catch these men responsible."

"That could take months. You don't even know who is after you guys and who killed those agents."

"Frederick Price is still alive."

Cody's mouth gaped open, and then he ran his fingers through his hair and paced.

"Oh, fuck. He wants you dead. You and the others destroyed that operation and confiscated all that money. He was the reason you were holding on to this job and not getting out. You wanted the agency to find him, and they would spend the money. What the fuck are they doing now that five agents are dead, including Williams? Huh? Are they fucking going to protect all of you?"

"Four agents didn't make it out of their undercover operations, and four are missing with no contact yet."

"Oh God, Jeremy. God damn it, this is the worst possible situation. We have to find Frederick Price and this hit man of his."

"We?" Jeremy asked.

"Fuck yeah. I'll use my connections, too. When is Spelling going to contact you?"

"Once he has an update and also has men look through our house."

Cody's eyes widened. "You think someone has been there or is there waiting to kill you?"

Jeremy felt the anger pool in his belly.

"Shit, Jeremy, what about those two flat tires you had? Could this guy have been fucking with you?"

When Cody said that, Jeremy thought about the boot prints on the front porch. His eyes widened. "He was already there." He then told Cody about the boot prints.

"If this guy tapped the lines, then he knows about us and that you're here. He could be in Treasure Town right now. We need help here, Jeremy. We have to protect our family."

He looked around the yard, suddenly feeling as if someone was watching them, and it pissed him off. He wasn't going to let Frederick Price and his hit man get away with this.

"It ends here, Cody. We have to find Price and this guy."

"Together. We'll do it together," Cody said, and Jeremy nodded just as Catalina opened the glass sliding door, smiling wide.

"Come on, you two. Dinner is ready, and dessert is in the oven."

She squealed as Cooper came up behind her, wrapped an arm around her waist, and pressed his hand under her skirt. "No, dessert is right here," Cooper said and suckled against her neck.

"Cooper," she scolded and laughed, pushing from him, turning around, and heading back inside.

Cody and Jeremy locked gazes. He had to protect his family, even if it meant giving up his life to do so.

Chapter 5

Jeremy held Catalina in his arms and kissed her deeply. He ran his hands along her ass and squeezed, loving how she looked in the nursing uniform. His heart was heavy because he knew he was leaving tonight to try and smoke this asshole—Clover, the agency believed the hit man's name was—out from under his rock. He could very well be in town just waiting to make a move.

He pulled from her lips and held her close. "I love you, Catalina. Be safe and text us to keep in touch."

She smiled. "I love you, too. I can't text you in the middle of the night while you're sleeping, silly, but I will as I'm leaving to head back here around seven or so, okay?" She kissed his lips and pulled back.

He didn't quite release her, and she looked at him as if something was wrong. He needed to give himself a mental shove to remind himself that this had to be done to protect her and his brothers. He smiled. "I'll miss you and that sexy body."

She blushed.

Cody kissed her next, and then Don and Cooper.

* * * *

Don and Jeremy joined Cody and Don in the living room.

"You guys have been acting so strange the last few days. You freaked out about Catalina working the night shift tonight, and even now, it's like you didn't want her out of your sight. What gives?" Cooper asked as he and Don sat on the couch in the living room.

Cody walked over toward his laptop, and Jeremy was looking at his cell phone.

"Hello, spill the fucking beans. Something is going on. You're both in protective military mode," Don added.

"We were going to talk to you about this when we had an update. There's some heavy shit going on," Cody said, and then Jeremy exhaled.

As he explained with every detail, Cooper felt his anger boiling and his upset about the situation get the better of him.

"Catalina won't understand about you leaving, Jeremy. This will hurt her and make her think this relationship won't work," he told him.

"Cooper, I can't risk getting you guys hurt or killed. This guy Clover is one badass fucking psycho killer. He's a hired hit man. I won't stand a chance, and neither will any of you if he decides to hunt me down here and kill me."

"Jesus, I wish you chose a fucking different profession. What the fuck?" Don exclaimed.

"This is him. Memorize his face, and if you see him in town, get Catalina and take off, then text me and let me know what's happening. Cerdic, Andreas, Gideon, and Lew know what's happening. They'll get you guys to a safe location and provide additional protection. Nate Hawkins has a hideout location a few hours up north, and it can be fully stocked within hours."

Cody turned the laptop screen toward Cooper and Don. Cooper swallowed hard. "That's the man who killed the agents and wants to kill you?" Don asked.

"Cody is working on things from his end. This guy Clover was at our house in New York. Some of the agents with the agency were sent there when Don and I started thinking about a few strange things that happened before we left to come here. The investigators found a bunch of things. He bugged the rooms, which means he knows about you guys and probably Catalina.

"In order to steer him away from you guys, I need to leave here and draw him out, someplace where I think I can get a look at him and turn this around. My agency is setting up a fake transaction at an isolated location where we can get this guy. Then Cody and his connections, along with my agency, will hopefully smoke out Frederick Price and we can end this shit once and for all."

"What if something goes wrong?" Cooper asked as Don sat there in silence, not saying a word.

Jeremy held his gaze and then looked at Don and Cody.

"I will do whatever is necessary to protect the three of you and our woman. I leave tonight."

"Tonight?" Don asked and gripped the arms of the couch. "This is going to get fucked up. We could lose you. You could get killed. We're going to lose Catalina. What do we tell her so she knows it isn't her and doesn't think that you don't love her and want this relationship?"

"You tell her the truth about me loving her and that something with my job is taking me away for a while. You're not sure how long, but it's all so that we can be together."

"I don't like this, Jeremy. You're heading into a gunfight blind," Don stated in anger.

"You think I want to do this? You think I want to leave you guys and Catalina and maybe get killed? I fucking don't. I'm sick with worry, Don. I've put you all in danger because of this fucking job and my obsession with finding Frederick and taking him down. He's pissed, and he's killed other agents. I could very well die, but I need to fight and try to resolve this. I have to end this before one of you gets hurt or killed because of me. I need your support right now, your strength to get through this so I can kill these two fucking men." He raised his voice and then ran his hands through his hair.

They were all quiet, and Don stood up.

"You've got my support." He hugged Jeremy. "I love you, bro. Don't go getting fucking killed on us, please. This family needs a leader, and you're it." He then pulled back.

"I don't plan on getting killed. I plan on doing the killing and protecting all of you. Stay strong and be sure to take care of Catalina while I'm gone."

"We will," Cooper said, but he couldn't help but feel that things were going to go wrong and his brother could get hurt or even killed. That just didn't sit right with him at all. How the hell was he going to keep the truth and his fear from Catalina?

* * * *

Catalina couldn't help it. Despite everything that Cody, Cooper, and Don told her about Jeremy having to leave for business, she felt their overprotectiveness full-force. She questioned them numerous times, and they denied anything was wrong and turned her fears and worry into kisses and bouts of lovemaking, but her gut told her they were lying, and she couldn't help but think that maybe Jeremy had changed his mind about wanting her.

As she tied her sneakers and prepared to race in the 10K, she looked up to see Cody, Cooper, and Don, along with her friends, Shayla, MaryAnne, and Destiny as well as Serefina, Michaela, Sophia, and their men as her own cheering crowd. She'd started spending a lot of time with Sophia and her men and couldn't help but feel as if they were watching over her, too.

In fact, yesterday at work, Lew had stopped in to see her and just say hello, which was odd. She saw him eying over some of the patients in the ER, and then she noticed that every night she worked, there was a deputy in there, as if on patrol.

She swallowed hard and then took a drink of water.

"Runners, take your places." The announcement came over the loud speaker, and the crowd cheered with encouragement for all of the people participating.

Catalina found her spot and took a few steady breaths. She glanced at her men, who gave her the thumbs-up and smiled. She had worked hard for this and really wanted to place.

The moment the gunshot went off indicating the start of the race, she took off with the large crowd. Some moved quickly, but she knew to pace herself and save the extra energy for the final miles. She had to focus on the run and getting to the finish line. She would worry about Jeremy and what really was going on later when she could question her men and get to the bottom of things.

* * * *

"Any word from Jeremy?" Lew asked Cody as they walked toward the trucks and the large-screen TV that tracked the racers and kept eyes on them the entire time.

"Nothing since he left. I'm so worried. Spelling hadn't heard anything, either."

"Well, we have our guys looking into any chatter and location on Frederick since he's been in contact with Clover. If we can get our hands on Clover's cell phone, then we can pinpoint a location on Frederick."

"Well, that will depend on a lot of factors, like if Clover follows Jeremy as he planned, and if Jeremy takes him down and can get that phone. They should be starting their show any day now. All we can do is wait," Cody said and then watched the screen, seeing Catalina pass a few runners and take position in tenth place.

Lew placed his hand on Cody's shoulder.

"We'll protect her. Everything will work out just fine. You'll see."

* * * *

Catalina couldn't believe it. She was pulling up into the third-place position on the final two miles of the race. It was all uphill before leading the straightaway through town by the boardwalk. The sun was beating down hard. Her legs were aching, and her chest felt tight as she gasped for air. She'd gone from wanting to place in the top ten to wanting to win the entire thing. She pumped her arms and passed the second-place runner and was side-by-side with the first-place runner. She didn't turn to look at the man. She just focused on the top of the hill and the descent down.

The crowds were cheering louder and louder. She felt the drive and need to win as the man pulled up a little ahead of her. She clenched her teeth and then heard him gasping for air and then slowing down slightly. He'd overexerted himself up the hill. Catalina pumped her arms faster, her feet pounding against the pavement. She heard the cheers, her name being yelled, and saw the lights of patrol cars flashing, their horns honking with encouragement from her crazy friends.

The finish line was straight ahead, and she didn't look back to see if the man or the others were on her tail. She pumped and pumped and gave her all as her chest slammed against the white ribbon over the finish line. Fire truck horns honked and sirens blared as she slowed down and then bent over, trying to catch her breath. A moment later, her men were lifting her up in the air and swinging her around, congratulating her. A swarm of her friends were there, too, and she felt the tears roll down her face. She'd done it. She'd run the race, and she'd won it all.

As she got hugs and kisses from them all, Cody handed her a bottle of water as Don placed a towel around her shoulders. She gripped onto Cooper so she wouldn't fall.

Then it hit her. Jeremy wasn't here to celebrate with her. Why was he really away? Was he in some sort of danger?

"Catalina?" Cody whispered and held her gaze as he cupped her face. "What's wrong?"

"I want to know the truth about Jeremy. I want to know why he couldn't be here, Cody. I want the truth," she said. Then Serefina and the girls all cheered and interrupted the moment, but one look at Cody, then the other men, and her heart felt heavy and more tears wanted to fall. Something was terribly wrong. She felt it in her chest and in her soul. Her men were deeply a part of her.

* * * *

Cody, Cooper, and Don watched Catalina sleep. She had been utterly exhausted after the race and taking a shower. The celebration at the Station was a lot of fun, but he could tell she had no more energy. She had demanded to know where Jeremy really was and they asked for some time to discuss it later tonight at home. She accepted their request because so many friends were around them and he thought she realized that what they would tell her required confidentiality. She was such a caring, big-hearted person. He felt guilty for not telling her everything right away.

Cody lifted her up and carried her out of the bar with their friends cheering, hooting, and hollering. Her large trophy would sit at the bar for a week, then move on to Sullivan's, then the ER, and finally her home. This was the first year in many that a citizen from Treasure Town had won first place in the race.

She lay in bed completely naked after they undressed her and helped her get ready for bed. She tried kissing Cody and talking him into making love, but as soon as she hit the pillow, she was out cold.

Cody caressed the hair from her cheek.

"She was amazing today. I was so proud of her and all she accomplished."

"You told her a dozen times, Cody. We all did. I can't even believe how amazing she was. That look in her eyes, the expression of determination on her face as she passed that guy and came running down the straightaway, taking first place. I felt tears in my eyes," Cooper admitted and smiled.

Don lay beside her on the bed, watching her.

"She's so special. She's a strong woman, maybe stronger than we've giving her credit for," Don said.

"We can't tell her, Don. It's how Jeremy wanted this," Cody said and stood up from the bed.

"Maybe she should know. That way she's on guard, too, when one of us isn't around to watch over her. Besides, we promised her we would discuss it at home, where it's safe. She deserves to know the truth." Cooper said to him.

"Hopefully we'll hear from Jeremy soon. Then he can explain himself and be here where he belongs."

"She was so upset today when it hit her that Jeremy wasn't there to witness her win like that."

"It was all recorded. He'll make it up to her when he comes back. Let's let her get some sleep. I have some work I need to do on the computer."

"Any updates at all, Cody?" Don asked.

Cody shook his head. "Something has to happen soon. I feel it. Something is going down. Let's pray that Jeremy is a step or two ahead."

* * * *

Jeremy's heart was pounding. He remained hidden as cars approached the warehouse and industrial building. The cars pulled up into the garage bays inside the building just as planned, and the agents got out. They were all inside the entryway of the warehouse. They were taking a huge risk by doing this, but Clover had gone after another agent and killed him. That led to information on another agent who seemed to be working for Frederick, too. He had been involved in the investigation during Sophia's abduction. He was the other snitch in the firm. They needed to take him out with Clover and hope there weren't others.

Agent Spelling had confided in Roger Clay, saying he needed a safe meeting point for Jeremy and wanted him to go in with another two agents, secure Jeremy, and provide protection for him and two other agents. This needed to end. They had a good idea of Frederick Price's location. He was somewhere in Pennsylvania, but they didn't have a definite locale. They were able to somewhat track Roger's cell phone and the calls he made from the agency and his private home line, but it gave them a fifty-mile radius of the area Price was hiding out in. They needed specifics. Once they killed Clover, they could get ahold of his cell phone and track the calls, or maybe get Roger Clay to talk.

"What's going on, Jones? Glad to see that you're still alive," Rogers said to him.

Jeremy held his gaze and pretended to be unaware of this rat bastard's true intentions. He couldn't help but think about the agents Rogers had helped Clover kill. Rogers deserved to die.

"Not as glad as I am. Do you have a plan and a safe house for us to go to?" Jeremy asked as he looked over at the other two agents.

"Sure do. If you want to follow me outside, we'll head out now. Don't want to be in one place too long," Rogers said.

Jeremy walked along with the other agents, his hand on his gun, prepared to fire, but they had a sniper on the roof and one in the woods in front. They would have a clear shot if Clover was there.

As they exited the building, they heard the shot. The sniper fell from the roof, and Jeremy and the others jumped to the protection of the car. More shots rang out, and Jeremy saw where they were coming from. As he looked at Rogers, he saw that Rogers was pointing a gun at him. The shot rang out, hitting Rogers in the chest. Another agent had killed him. Jeremy ran toward the safety of the warehouse, figuring he could run around back and come up to Clover from behind. More gunfire rang out, and he hurried, chest pounding, gun drawn as he ran across the clearing to the woods. He saw the flashes of light as Clover shot up the car and anyone near it.

"Put down your gun," he yelled to Clover. Clover turned and shot. Jeremy fired his weapon, shooting Clover between the eyes.

"It's over asshole, and your boss is next."

* * * *

Catalina was glad she was working the night shift. It had given her all day to rest up after the long run. She couldn't help but to smile. Everyone was coming in congratulating her and praising her win, but her heart was heavy. She got Cody to explain a little about Jeremy's absence. It was obvious that he was in danger. He was trying to protect her and his brothers and pull any potential danger away from them. As Cody explained, giving only some details of the case, she realized the seriousness of it and the fact that agents were being killed and Jeremy was being hunted. That explained why Lew and the deputies were continuously around the ER and why her men were being overprotective and not allowing her to go anywhere without them and protection.

Now she worried even more about Jeremy. What if he got hurt or was killed? What if she never saw him again? She felt the tears reach her eyes, and then took a deep breath and released it. She remembered Cody's words, and Cooper and Don's encouragement.

"You're a strong woman," Cody had told her. "You know right from wrong and about justice needing to be served. We're your men, and Jeremy and I have jobs that are dangerous where we deal with very evil people. You need to be strong and to know that we will always protect you and keep you out of harm's way. Jeremy is doing that now, Catalina, and you need to be aware and diligent as you live your life here. I don't want to scare you, but these men are resourceful. If you see anything suspicious or feel like something isn't right, just text or call us, and we'll come check it out. We don't care if it's nothing. You're a fighter and you're strong. You're made for us and us for you. Jeremy will be back, and we can move on with our future together."

She felt that inner need to be strong and be the woman they needed her to be.

Catalina looked at the clock. It was three a.m., and the ER was pretty quiet. There were three patients inside, one with chest pains, one who'd broke his arm in a drunken stupor as he tripped over a curb outside a bar in town, and the other was having abdominal pains and the doctor had determined it could be his appendix. They were bringing him up to X-rays when Catalina noticed the deputy wasn't sitting in his chair. Catalina walked into the hallway to see where he was, and he wasn't there, nor was the head nurse at the front desk. The doors to the ER room opened, which led from the main hallway into the hospital. It was an entrance doctors and nurses used. She saw a man coming inside, his head hung down, and he was moaning.

Without a second thought, she went to him.

"Do you need help, sir?" she asked.

He looked up, his eyes dark and his expression evil as he looked at her and smiled like he had succeeded in tricking her. Her gut clenched and she instantly felt the need to run, and to get away from him and call one of her men. She went to step back, but he grabbed her arm and pressed the gun to her side.

"Make any noise, and I'll kill you right here where your boyfriend can find you."

She knew right away he was talking about Jeremy, and she gasped, the fear hitting her belly.

She looked around frantically and then right at the camera. "Jeremy, help me," she lipped to it, and he pulled her from the ER out the emergency entrance and into the night.

She struggled once they were outside, thinking no one could get hurt but her at this point, but then came the prick to her neck. She gasped as he shoved her into the van.

"I heard about your spunk. I came prepared, Catalina. Your boyfriend took away everything that means anything to me. He took it all, and I have nothing. I'm a wanted man. Now I'm going to take everything from him."

She felt her head begin to ache, and her vision blurred just as she hit the metal floor of the van. She heard the door close, and then another door open and close, and then the engine start. She rolled as the van took off, and then she passed out completely.

* * * *

The sirens blared, putting the whole hospital on high alert as police and federal agents swarmed the building, trying to locate Frederick Price and Catalina.

Don looked at Cody and Cooper as information came flooding in. Deputy Davie Lee had been shot and was in critical condition. The head nurse had suffered a concussion. They now stood by the nurses' station looking at the surveillance video. Apparently the security guards had been in their office when it all went down and they were locked in, the door secured from the outside. Their quick thinking sent calls into the sheriff's department fast, but not fast enough to catch the van before it headed out of town.

They had helicopters in the air, and the agents were giving Cody and the sheriff updates on Jeremy and the team.

"They took out Clover two hours ago. Frederick must have found out and set this plan in motion. He's desperate, and he wants revenge. Jeremy uncovered the snitch in the agency. He's dead now, too."

"Jesus, this is a fucking mess," Lew said to them.

"We have to find that van and get to Catalina before this asshole kills her," Don stated.

Cody's phone rang.

"It's Jeremy," he said and answered it.

"The setup worked. We know where Frederick is, and we're headed there. This will be over soon."

"He's got Catalina," Cody told his brother.

"What? How the fuck did that happen? What do you mean?" he carried on, and Cody explained. He heard his brother yelling, and then he clamed down.

"I'm going to kill this fucking guy. How long ago did this happen?"

"Thirty minutes."

"Fuck. He must be heading to Pennsylvania. Are their eyes in the sky?"

"Yes, and I've got my guys in motion to use their special skills. I hope to have a location on that van any minute."

"Okay, we're headed that way. Let me know the moment you get a location."

"You got it, Jeremy." Cody rubbed his hand along his jaw. "We have to find that van and fast. He's going to kill her."

"We've got men tracking the phone calls, and we've come up with three separate locations where he could be headed," the federal agent told them.

"Then we need to plan a simultaneous raid on all three locations once we ensure Catalina is safe and we can go in. If we hit the wrong place, he'll know and he'll kill her. We have to do this right. He's a fucking psycho, and this is definitely his line of thinking," Cody told them.

"Let's do it," Lew said, and they all started organizing their teams as they waited on confirmation of the three locations and the appearance of that van.

* * * *

Jeremy gripped the steering wheel so tightly. He wanted to kill Frederick. How the fuck had that asshole gotten to Catalina? He'd been so close to catching him and taking him out just like they had Clover and the snitch Rogers. That asshole Rogers had sold out his own men, his country, to the corrupt, murdering trash that Frederick was. How many agents had died, how many families left without a father, a husband a boyfriend, a son? Men like this needed to be eliminated and destroyed.

He was tired of this shit, tired of placing his life on the line and now sacrificing his own family because of this job. This shit had to stop. God, what if Catalina died? It would be all his fault. He should have stayed and protected his family and let the other agents take down Rogers and Clover. She wouldn't be in danger, and both men would be dead because the other agents were more than capable of doing the job. They'd lost their friends, their fellow agents, too.

He exhaled and felt his heart ache. *Please keep Catalina alive and let us get to her in time. I'm done with this life, this job. I need to focus on my family. Nothing else is more important. Nothing.*

* * * *

Catalina shivered. She blinked her eyes open and saw a man standing by a table. A bright light blinded her for a moment. Her head was pounding and her vision blurry, but she could see the metal devices, knives and other tools on a table, and a round container of fire. He was running the instruments across it. She shook, her body seemingly in shock from whatever he had injected into her skin.

She was slowly becoming more aware of the situation and the fact that she was lying on the floor in her panties and bra. Her lips felt sore, her cheekbone, too, and she wondered if he'd hit her. She started to move, but her limbs were weak, and she fell back down.

He turned to look at her.

"Good, you're awake. I was thinking I would have to do the rest while you were unconscious. That wouldn't be as much fun. I want to hear you scream for mercy, beg to be saved, and we're running out of time."

"Who are you, and why are you doing this to me?"

He picked up the knife and ran it over the flame, heating it.

"It doesn't matter who I am. Just know that the pain I'm going to cause you is because of your boyfriend, Agent Jones."

She felt the tears reach her eyes, and her heart pounded. She knew he was going to cut her, burn her flesh as he stabbed her or something. She lifted up, determined to fight her way out of this or die. Jeremy would eventually find him and kill him. She was on her own. She had to fight for her life.

He lowered to a squatting position over her legs.

"It will only hurt for a little while, and then the pain will be so bad you'll pass out, but then I'll wake you, and we'll start again." His eyes were so evil she felt he wasn't human at all, but some monster. This was the kind of man Jeremy had to hunt down in his career as an agent. No wonder he didn't want to quit. He probably feared more men like this would exist if he weren't there to kill them.

But where was he? Did he even know she'd been taken? Where the hell were they, anyway?

She took a few unsteady breaths and panicked as his hand came down on her thigh.

"You're very beautiful, but you won't be once I'm finished with you."

She struck him across the mouth, and he staggered back. She pulled herself up to her knees, fighting the weakness and the dull pounding in her head as he swung the knife at her chest. She fell back, causing him to miss, but then he grabbed her leg, pulled her forward, and stabbed down at her shoulder. She cried out as the pain radiated through her body, suddenly awakening her entirely, erasing the fog and replacing it with pure adrenaline.

She shoved at him, sending him flying into the table, knocking over the container of fire and some kind of liquid. It caught fire, quickly spreading around them.

She grabbed for whatever weapon she could as he came at her again like some raving lunatic.

She swung the metal with the sharp, hook-like edge and cut his chest, slicing through his shirt smooth and quick. His arm made contact with her face, and she fell back. The pain hit her face then her shoulder and back as she landed on the concrete flooring. The fire was spreading fast, and she jumped up and ran.

"You won't get away from me. No one can find you. You'll die out there."

He threw something at her, and it hit her arm, cut her skin, and made her stumble on the stairs.

"Get away from me!" she screamed and kicked at him, knocking him down a few steps.

She shoved open the door at the top of the stairs. The place was in complete darkness, the only light coming from the moon outside. She felt around the wall, then heard the door slam open and him yelling.

"I'll find you. I'll kill you, bitch. I'll cut you to fucking pieces and leave you here for all those fucking agents to see. They'll never catch me and kill me."

She was crying, but trying to be quiet. *Where's the door? Oh God, please let me get out of here.* She felt the pain radiate against her shoulder. She was bleeding so much. She knew she needed to get a move on it and get out of here. She could go into shock from the stab wound. She eased slowly down the wall. He was banging open doors and heading the opposite way. She was barefoot, wearing only panties and a bra, but she had to run. She needed to get out of the house and run.

She saw him, the shadow of a man, and he had a gun. She was going to die. It was run and take the chance to live and escape, or stay here and suffer a horrible death.

She was shaking harder, and she knew it was bad. She could go into shock, and then she wouldn't be able to move at all. She looked around frantically and saw the doorway. She made her way toward it and began to open the door.

She screamed as the shot rang out, hitting the wood by her head. She pulled the door open and slammed it behind her as she headed to the right, ducking and weaving. It was complete darkness out there, like they were in the woods somewhere. She ran toward the trees, her feet aching and broken branches, rocks, and sharp sticks cutting into her skin painfully.

More shots rang out, just missing her, and she tried not to scream and hoped he was just taking potshots and couldn't see her, but she heard his boots crushing the branches on the ground. She looked over her shoulder as she continued to run and her chest slammed into a tree, scraping her breasts and her arm. She gasped and fell to her knees, then hurried to get up.

"Oh God, please. Please, someone help me."

Another shot rang out. "I'm getting closer, bitch. You're gonna die," he yelled, and she saw a flash of light to the right and then heard the roar of vehicles. Was that a chopper in the distance?

Strong arms grabbed her around her midsection, pulling her toward a thick, hard chest.

She screamed.

"Catalina, it's me. It's Cody."

She hugged him tightly and heard the grunts and the yelling, and then shots fired. She shook as Cody held her tightly. He was dressed in black, a mask hiding half his face, and she felt the utility belt against her hips. His arm and gun pointed toward the darkness.

She was hysterically crying against his shoulder, trying to be quiet, but the adrenaline rush was dissipating and she was going into shock.

"He's dead. I got him," she heard Jeremy yell, and then the place illuminated with lights from Jeeps and trucks as well as the helicopter from above. The sound of the rotors had her heart pounding.

"Oh God, baby, you're okay. My God, are you all right?"

"Shock...shhhhock." Her voice quivered.

"Fuck, I need help here. She's going into shock," Cody yelled.

"Lay her down on this blanket," Lew said, appearing with other men, who were all dressed in black, holding guns and looking like some special operations unit.

She blinked her eyes opened and closed.

"Pressure to the knife wound," she said, breathing heavily.

"Knife wound?" Jeremy asked as he knelt down and caressed her cheek.

"She's cut on the shoulder. It's deep. I need something to stop the bleeding," Cody stated.

"Pressure, Cody. Hold it tight. I can take it." She swallowed hard.

"Get me something to cover her up. She'll freeze out here, and she's in shock. We need to keep her warm," Cody said, and then someone brought over a federal agent jacket they'd taken off to give to her.

"The chopper can land in the clearing and take her to the ER. We need to pick her up," Lew told Cody and Jeremy.

"All right. Nice and easy. Baby, we have to pick you up," Cody told her.

"Just do it," she stated firmly, and Lew chuckled.

Catalina felt her vision begin to blur again. "I'm going to pass out, Cody. Keep the pressure on and keep me warm," she said, slurring her words.

"Yes, ma'am," Cody stated, and she closed her eyes as she felt herself being lifted into the helicopter, the sound of the rotors so loud yet relaxing as she focused on the sound.

She could hear the radio echo in the background and then felt the hands holding hers, and she knew Cody and Jeremy were with her.

She smelled fire in the distance, smoke in the air, and heard sirens blaring, and then there was silence.

* * * *

Jeremy sat in the chair next to Catalina's bed in the hospital. She was all bruised up from head to toe from fighting for her life. He almost hadn't made it to her in time. It had been too close and too upsetting to think about. He thought about the way they got to her and how she'd been running through the woods as Frederick took shots at her. She had a stab wound that required surgery and a lot of stitches, bruising and cuts to her face, her chest, and her feet, and she had gone into shock on the helicopter. It had been so frightening, too frightening to think about what life would be without her.

But things were going to be different now. He'd given his resignation and would hook up with Nate and Lew's connections for some private contracts and investigative work when he was ready. His only focus was loving Catalina, taking care of her as she healed and enjoying their lives together in Treasure Town.

He glanced at Cody, who leaned back in the chair and just stared at her.

"When is she going to wake up and stay awake for a while? I miss her voice," he said, and Jeremy nodded.

"I do, too, but the doctors said it could take some time for her body to heal after all the trauma. She's bruised up everywhere."

The door to the room opened, and Cooper and Don appeared, carrying coffee and some snacks.

"How is she?" Cooper asked as he handed out the coffee cups.

"She hasn't awoken again since this morning," Jeremy said and then took a sip of the coffee, feeling the need for some caffeine to keep him awake. They'd spent the last several days here and taken turns showering at a friend's house who lived near the hospital. As soon as she was well enough, the doctors said they could transfer to

Treasure Town and the Fairway General Hospital there. They were about an hour from there.

Jeremy heard her moan, and he quickly stood up and went closer to the bed. The others joined him, and Cooper caressed her cheek.

"Hey, sleepy head. We've been waiting to see those baby blues."

She blinked her eyes open, looked at them, and smiled softly, then cringed. Cooper caressed her chin.

"Easy, baby. Lots of bruises, remember?"

They talked to her and told her how much they missed her voice as she managed to focus more than the last time she'd awoken, and then wanted to sit up. Jeremy raised the bed slowly. She crinkled her nose and then used her good arm to cover her belly. The other arm and shoulder were in a sling and all bandaged up.

"Ah, someone is awake. How are you feeling, Catalina?" the doctor asked as he walked into the room, along with a nurse.

"Nauseous," she whispered and swallowed hard.

"That's probably from the pain medication and not eating regular food."

"Well, can we stop the pain meds? I want to wake up and get better."

"Honey, you were stabbed, and you're bruised all over the place," Jeremy told her. She glanced at him.

"I'm not sleeping my life away. I can handle a little pain. I want to be awake...talk to you guys."

The doctor smiled.

"Let's lower the dosage. If you can get down some soup or a little food, then we'll see."

She nodded. "Thank you," she whispered and closed her eyes.

"Here, suck on a little bit of ice while Don gets you food," Cooper told her, and Jeremy watched as they all took care of their woman, who seemed to finally be getting better. He couldn't want to get her home where they could hold her in their arms and love her forever.

Chapter 6

Catalina sat on the stool at the Station talking to Michaela, Serefina, Sophia, Shayla, and Destiny while MaryAnn spoke to some guys who were friends of Jeremy's from the agency.

She was so happy that she'd survived the ordeal and that Jeremy and her men were safe, too. They'd all told her about the strategic operations between numerous government agencies to find her and plan the rescue. She'd had to get debriefed by some federal agents and other people to document the events. That was all behind her now, and her shoulder was feeling a lot better every day, especially with Cody and Jeremy showing her exercises to do and ways to work out the aches. She especially liked when those sessions turned into making love on the living room rug.

"Hey, Catalina, do you need another drink?" C.C. asked her, and she smiled.

"I'm good for now. Thank you." Catalina wondered about the young woman who worked at the Station and what her story was. She seemed so sad, and Catalina would catch her watching them and smiling as if she was envious. So she made an effort to talk to her a little, and each time, C.C. seemed to be letting her guard down and smiling more.

"So, you've got yourself four very amazing men, but have they decided on the house they want to buy or what?" Serefina asked, and Michela and Shayla chuckled.

"I don't know why they're being so particular. Everything you've shown us has been great, and the first house and the third house were gorgeous," she replied.

"There's a lot to be said for a beach house right on the water with your own private stretch of beach," Sophia added, then took a sip from her wine glass.

"It's completely up to them," Catalina said and then covered her mouth as she yawned.

"Are we boring you?" Serefina teased.

"Not at all. I think I'm finally starting to relax a little. You know, feeling comfortable and safe again."

"I'm sure that has a lot to do with your men. Who are on the way over right now," Shayla said as she slid off the bar stool, waved, and then headed toward their other friends.

Jeremy pulled her into a hug and kissed her neck, but looked at Serefina. "Ladies, if you don't mind, we're going to call it a night. We've got a big day tomorrow."

"Really? What's going on?" Catalina asked.

He pulled back, and Cody, Cooper and Don joined them

"We're going to be meeting with Sophia at the real estate office to sign contracts on our house," Jeremy said.

"Really?" both Catalina and Sophia asked and then chuckled.

"Which one?" Catalina asked.

"You'll find out tomorrow," Cody told her, and then took her hand and helped her down off the stool.

They said their good-byes and headed out of the Station as their friends and fellow community members acknowledged them and smiled.

"I love living in Treasure Town. I'm so glad that we're staying here," she told Cooper as she snuggled against his side.

"There's no place we'd rather be than here with you and all our friends," Cody told her.

Cooper kept her close. Cody held her hand, and Jeremy and Don walked along with them. The night was cool and pleasant as they made their way to the parking lot, the smell of the ocean in the air and peace all around her.

She thought about how they'd first met and how Jeremy had been shot trying to help rescue Sophia. Their paths hadn't crossed again for months because it hadn't been the right time or the right place, but as fate stepped in and brought them together, the timing became perfect. Like her friends, she had to fight for her love, question whether it was right, or would last, until she focused on the most obvious method of figuring it out. She followed her heart.

She remembered from day one meeting them in the ER and feeling her heart warm and her insides react. One look, a few exchanged words, and, indeed, they'd set her heart on fire. It was a flame that would burn forever, because true love had the power to make it through everything.

THE END

WWW.DIXIELYNNDWYER.COM

ABOUT THE AUTHOR

People seem to be more interested in my name than where I get my ideas for my stories from. So I might as well share the story behind my name with all my readers.

My momma was born and raised in New Orleans. At the age of twenty, she met and fell in love with an Irishman named Patrick Riley Dwyer. Needless to say, the family was a bit taken aback by this as they hoped she would marry a family friend. It was a modern day arranged marriage kind of thing and my momma downright refused.

Being that my momma's families were descendants of the original English speaking Southerners, they wanted the family blood line to stay pure. They were wealthy and my father's family was poor.

Despite attempts by my grandpapa to make Patrick leave and destroy the love between them, my parents married. They recently celebrated their sixtieth wedding anniversary.

I am one of six children born to Patrick and Lynn Dwyer. I am a combination of both Irish and a true Southern belle. With a name like Dixie Lynn Dwyer it's no wonder why people are curious about my name.

Just as my parents had a love story of their own, I grew up intrigued by the lifestyles of others. My imagination as well as my need to stray from the straight and narrow made me into the woman I am today.

Enjoy *Hearts on Fire 7: Claiming Catalina* and allow your imagination to soar freely.

For all titles by Dixie Lynn Dwyer, please visit
www.bookstrand.com/dixie-lynn-dwyer

Siren Publishing, Inc.
www.SirenPublishing.com

Lightning Source UK Ltd.
Milton Keynes UK
UKOW06f2338130616

276264UK00020B/469/P